Everything Is Alright

Everything Is Alright

Kelli Rajala

Everything Is Alright

Kelli Rajala

2024

Everything Is Alright

This is a work of fiction. Unless otherwise indicated, all the names, characters, businesses, places, evens, and incidents in this book are either the product of the author's imagination or used in a fictitious manner. Any resemblance to actual persons, living or dead, or actual events is purely coincidental.

First Printing: 2024

ISBN 9798884849556

www.facebook.com/Kerajala41

Kelli Rajala

Everything Is Alright

To all of my friends, family, teachers, and anyone else who has ever supported my writing endeavors.

To all the people who have been willing to share their own stories.

Thank you!

Everything Is Alright

Chapter One

Today is my first day at my first real "adult" job. I pre-planned my outfit last week, made sure to get my hair freshly cut, and also got a new bag to carry all of my stuff in, one that looks more professional. This job is full-time and I have actual benefits. No more retail, no more 10-15 hours per week living paycheck to paycheck and debating whether or not I *really* need that loaf of bread. I have a real job. I have a job I'm excited to be going to for once.

I'll admit that I still feel a little out of place when I pull up into the parking lot. My car has a little more rust than everyone else's and an exhaust leak that makes it on the louder side. The thing is, my car is almost as old as I am. It sticks out amongst the much newer models surrounding me, but that's okay. I can save up now.

When I walk into the office I'm greeted by my fellow receptionist, Sarah. She's not much older than me, very friendly, and the first time we met we really hit it off, so I think working together will be a breeze.

"I'll go let Erik know you're here!" she tells me excitedly.

Erik is my new boss. He's super chill, super friendly, and super gay. Sarah has already let me know that his husband, Jeff, will be coming in to see him often, so I can let Jeff walk back to his office without question. There are actually a few people who come often enough that I'll have to start remembering them, as most of my coworkers are married and/or have children. Yet another way that I don't fit in.

Erik comes out from his office in the back and offers me his hand to shake. He's a whole foot taller than my tiny five-foot frame, so I have to look up quite a bit to meet his gaze. I'd say he's kinda cute, too, in a mildly feminine sort of way, with blonde hair and hazel eyes framed by long lashes. I'm sure he gets hit on by women more often than he'd like. You know… before they find out.

"Hey! Good to see you again," he says. "Ready to jump right in?"

I let out a nervous sort of laugh. It's one of the busier times of the year for the Southern Michigan University Admissions office.

"I suppose I'll have to be."

He chuckles.

"That's okay! Sarah here will be the one training you," he tells me, nodding in her direction, "and she's practically a pro at this now."

"*Ha*! Right. Thanks for that vote of confidence, though," she says.

"She's just humble. Anyway, I'd like to go over some things with you first, mostly housekeeping and general new hire stuff. Nothing scary. If you would please follow me back to my office."

The day continues as one might expect their first day to. A whole lot of talking, paperwork, and getting accounts set up. Not a lot of actual work. I am able to answer the phone since most calls need to be transferred elsewhere anyway, but Sarah is currently balancing literally everything else on her own. I suppose I shouldn't be surprised. She's been doing this alone all summer since the last woman quit.

I watch her greet visitors, answer questions, help with directions, do the paperwork, the picking up and distributing of mail, and also answering the phone. Today is no slow day, either. We have no chairs left in our lobby for people to sit and there isn't enough room to add more, leaving people to have to stand.

Some of the visitors come up to me and start rattling questions off and I am embarrassed to tell them I don't know the answers yet. They're nice, though. They understand. For some reason the people on the phones, however, aren't always as understanding.

"SMU Admissions, this is Charlie. How can I help you?"

(Insert long conversation with a woman who was mad at me for not having all the answers.) Eventually, and thankfully, I remember that I can transfer her to a counselor and hang up the phone, so I do just that, breathing a sigh of relief.

When I turn to the front of my desk, there's a man standing on the other side, watching me.

"By the look on your face," he says, "I'd say that was a difficult one?"

I sigh, ready to start venting to a complete stranger, because why not? Although, maybe that's not such a good idea. He could be a visitor, and I'm pretty sure venting to visitors is unprofessional.

And then I actually look *at* him.

And *oh my, God.*

"What do you want, Noah?" Sarah asks before I can say anything.

He hands her a paper.

"Can you look this person up for me? See if they actually plan on coming in the fall?"

"Sure thing."

He turns back to me.

This man has the most beautifully green eyes I have ever seen on a human being in real life. No photo editing. I realize he's talking again, but my brain has stopped processing what's being said.

"You alright?" he finally asks.

Thankfully my brain actually catches this.

I nod.

"Yes. Sorry. I'm new here. Though… I guess you already know that, because it's pretty obvious. I mean you wouldn't have seen me here before. Uh… I'm sorry."

Oh no. Brain. Please don't fail me.

Noah laughs softly and it's such a soothing sound.

"Yeah. I may have picked up on that." He holds his hand out. "Noah Foster. I work next door in Financial Aid. I come here quite regularly and I know I have never seen you before…" He glances quickly at my name plate. "Charlie Cooper."

"They're not coming."

We both look over in Sarah's direction, seemingly having forgotten that she was looking something up for him. Right. She hands the paper back to him.

"That's what I thought," he says as he grabs it from her. "Thank you very much." He turns to me again, those intense green eyes piercing straight into the very depths of my soul. "Nice meeting you, Charlie."

I like the way it sounds when he says my name.

"N-nice uh… meeting you too."

The words stumble awkwardly out of my mouth. Once he's gone, I can feel my cheeks burning. I imagine they must be as red as tomatoes. Sarah laughs beside me.

"What?" I ask.

"Yeah, he's cute, ain't he?"

The burn grows stronger.

"Uh... no... I mean yeah, but... i-it's not... I wasn't...."

The sentence trails off as I realize I have nothing to say back to that. He *is* cute. He has short brown hair, just long enough to suggest it hasn't been cut in a while. It gives him an almost boyish quality even with the facial hair. He can't be too much older than me. I'm sure of it. Not that it matters, obviously. I did not come here to find myself a boyfriend. I came here to work.

Sarah laughs again.

"Relax. You're not alone. Just about every woman in this office has a crush on him. Even Anna, who I'm sure is old enough to be the man's mother. You wouldn't be the first one to notice that he's a good-looking guy. I know Erik thinks he's cute, too. He just won't admit it."

"How long has he been here?"

"I believe about eight years. Three longer than me."

"He looks young to have been here that long."

She shrugs.

"He started relatively soon after he graduated with his Master's from here. So yeah, I think he's somewhere in his mid-thirties."

"Well... it doesn't matter anyway," I finally say.

"Do you already have a boyfriend? Husband?"

"No," I tell her. "I am so single it's... not something I laugh about anymore," I admit. "I'm 30 years old. At this rate I'm going to die alone."

She gives me a wink.

"You never know. I'm pretty sure he's still single."

I roll my eyes.

"Yeah. Right. He's also way out of my league. Men like that don't like women like me. I'm just... meh."

"Are you kidding? You're *so* pretty. You have no idea how much I wish I could pull off mint green hair the way you do. Brown is so boring."

I don't know. I've never really considered myself to be particularly pretty. More average than anything. And beautiful men like Noah do not go for average women like me. I'm sure he'll end up with some blonde, long-legged, skinny, model type. I mean, I'm not overweight by any means. I know that. But I do have a little bit of extra belly fat I'd really like to burn off. I'm short. My face is okay, but there are definitely things about it I wish I could change.

There are also other things. Things about me I don't like, but we'll get into that later. All in all, I'm 100% certain that Noah would not go for someone like me. Not that I want that. I'm not here to find a man. I've already established that.

Get it together, Charlie. You've been here for less than one *day.*

Everything Is Alright

Chapter Two

I'm so happy to finally have a place to myself, but getting home to an empty apartment can feel pretty lonely. All the lights are off. Everything's closed up. I need to get a cat or something.

I drop my bag and flop down on my bed. Today went by quickly, which is nice. I was introduced to all of my coworkers that I didn't get to meet when I came for my interview. They all seem like really nice people. Everyone in this office gets along so well. It feels strange, since I'm used to working places where at least two people hate each other. It's quite refreshing, really.

However, there's one person that I can't get out of my head and he doesn't even work in our office. He has nothing to do with my job, which is what today is supposed to be about. It's my first real step into actual adulthood after all.

But those eyes.

That's the part I truly can't get out of my head. That and his soft voice and adorable smile.

Noah.

“Why do you have this effect on me?” I ask the empty room. “We literally met for like… two whole minutes.”

I close my eyes. I have a slight headache from the overload of information I’ve been bombarded with today. There’s no way I’m going to remember even half of it by tomorrow morning. Maybe I should have taken more notes. I make a mental note to do so tomorrow.

My phone buzzes on the bed next to me. When I pick it up and look at it I have missed messages from seven different people.

“Ugh. I don’t feel like answering you all back right now,” I say, and then drop my phone back on my bed. *I’m too tired.*

I know it’s all friends and family asking how my first day went. I’ll give them an update later. Right now, I want to nap, so I get up off my bed and change into a comfy pair of pajamas. I’ll just take a quick nap, then make dinner.

Except I don’t take a quick nap.

I fall asleep for roughly two and a half hours. When I wake up it’s already almost 7:30 PM and I feel groggy instead of rested. Regardless, I need to eat food, which means dinner ends up being a bowl of cereal since it requires no effort to make. I eat in front of the TV and turn on some show I don’t have to fully give my attention to. All seven people are still waiting for a response. Some of them are now starting to wonder where I am and why

I'm not answering. I suppose I'll have to get back to those people first.

All the lights in my apartment are off except for a small lamp in my bedroom, so the only bright light is the flickering from the TV. Everything's quiet, especially since so far I have yet to see one of my neighbors. I know they exist. I see the cars. I see the names on the mailboxes downstairs. Just no people yet.

It's better than my last place where my next-door neighbors partied all the time and the hallway constantly smelled like weed. My roommate never cleaned anything and was rarely ever home alone, if you know what I mean. My last apartment was definitely more suited for college students, but at the time it was the only thing I could afford. I worked in retail making barely over minimum wage. You get what you pay for and all.

This place I'm in now is small, but it's home. I have everything I need. I've lived here for a little over a month now and finally have things set up the way I want them. Art on the walls. Dishes washed and put away. Laundry taken care of. I also bought a bunch of stuff to make my bathroom cute, because, you know, priorities. All in all, I'm off to a good start. Whether or not I can keep things this way is to be determined.

After I'm done eating and replying to people, I take a bubble bath. This is just what I need after a hectic day of training and people and information. My stiff muscles feel better in the hot, soapy water. The steam clears my sinuses a little. I could fall asleep here if I'm not careful.

There's music playing through my stereo via Bluetooth since all my music is on my phone. It's handy. I don't have to get up to change a song, I can just swipe to a new one. Perfect for taking a bath.

I don't even bother turning on the bathroom light. Instead I leave my bathroom door open and let the glow from a lamp be the only source. It's more relaxing this way. And I need to relax.

Because I'm still kind of thinking about Noah right now.

Oh, God.

No.

I cannot think about him while I'm naked in a tub. It feels wrong. It feels dirty somehow.

If you were to ask me what I'm most attracted to in people, though, what catches my attention first, my answer would be their eyes. It's always been that way.

The thing is… words and actions can be manipulated to suit someone's needs, their ulterior motive. They can lie. They can trick. I have found, however, that it's often difficult for people to lie with their eyes. The eyes can show whether or not someone is truthful, even if they try to hide it in every other way. We just don't have as much control over what our eyes show other people. Plus, they're pretty colors. Who doesn't like pretty colors?

I get out of the tub and put on newer pajamas since it feels wrong to think about putting on the pair I had just been wearing, even though they weren't actually dirty. It's a thing. I'm really particular about feeling clean.

Back to eyes, though. Mine are blue. This seems to be the most popular color, the most written about, sung about, and what have you, but I don't think they're special. I don't see why so many people want them. They're not the prettiest after all. Coincidentally, my favorite eye color is and always has been green.

Green eyes and brown hair.

The more I think about it, the more I realize Noah fits the description of all of the fantasy men I've imagined myself with over the years. Same hair color. Same eye color. Same build really. I'd say he's kind of average in that sense, maybe a little more on the fit side. He definitely looks like he must be an active person, but he's not all big muscles. In fact, he's on the smaller side. He is literally what I've always wanted.

I'm not that lucky, though. I never have been. I don't get what I want. Ever. I don't win drawings and can just forget about the lottery. I never get the guy. (I have had boyfriends, but they were both jerks and that was all the way back in high school so it doesn't even count.) Admittedly, I was also mostly in it just to say I had a boyfriend. And I know that sounds bad, but like, I was a teenager. Not a very smart one at that.

I struggled through school. It's actually a miracle that I have a Bachelor's degree, since I almost didn't even graduate from high school, and it took way longer to earn than it should have due to struggles with mental health. I've hated all my previous jobs. No car I've ever had has lasted me more than two years. Yeah. I think I've painted the picture well enough to prove my point about my odds with Noah.

It's not even like I know anything about him. He could be a serial killer. He could be a collector of clown dolls. He could be both of those things, because honestly, they seem like they would go hand-in-hand. He could actually just be a huge jerk. Who's to say? He may have the looks I've always pictured, but his personality could be the exact opposite. How else is he still single?

Of course, he does have a Master's degree, and he works in one of the more difficult offices to work in on campus. He was apparently hired pretty young, so I know he's smart and must have made a good impression with his work ethic. I wonder what he went to school for.

I majored in art and design. You can see how great of an idea that was considering I work somewhere that has absolutely nothing to do with anything I got out of that degree, but whatever. I already wasn't a good student. I didn't want to go to school for something I didn't like just because it would end up making me more money. I don't live my life always thinking about a bigger paycheck. In fact, my new job definitely does not pay as much as it should, but I don't care. I like it. That's what's important to me.

I just want to be *happy*.

Everything Is Alright

Chapter Three

The only thing I *don't* particularly like about my job is going in for 7:30 AM. It'll change to 8:00 for the school year, but honestly, what's a half hour? I'd rather be in bed until noon. Instead, here I am, washing my hair and getting dressed and getting all of my things together in the short twenty minutes I've allowed for myself to get ready.

What makes 7:30 AM even less fun is how chipper everyone else seems to be. What is wrong with these people? Do they not need sleep? There must be something wrong with them.

Okay, that's harsh. All of my coworkers seem like great people. I'm just moody in the morning.

Thankfully, we have quite a few people coming in for visits most days. It's good to be kept busy, otherwise I'm just sitting here reading through a binder about various procedures whenever Sarah doesn't have something specific for me to be doing. And reading out of a binder will really tempt me to nod off.

"Good morning! Sleep well?" Sarah asks as soon as I walk through the door.

"Yeah. I think it helps getting back into a routine. In the time I spent without a job my sleep schedule was awful."

"Yeah, I know how that can get. Last time I had a vacation you'd think I didn't know one day from the next when I got back." Sarah walks over and hands me a stack of papers. "These are from last week, but I've saved them so you can learn what to do. It's just basic data entry stuff."

I take the stack from her. It's at least an inch thick.

"Seems like a lot," I point out.

"Oh, no. Don't worry. You don't have to enter all of this. There're just a few things from each sheet that need to be put into our system. We like to keep track of prospective students that visit for tours and counselor meetings and all that. Most of the other information is already entered anyway."

"Oh. Okay."

She shows me where to go and where to enter the information and what information needs to be entered.

I can't lie, most of my job isn't all that exciting. I could sit here and talk about data entry all day, but that doesn't mean anyone would want to listen. I know that. I mean I do also bring the mail down and pick it up… which is equally as exciting.

-

This is essentially how my entire first week goes, plus the occasional meeting with my boss to go over some more things that should help get me situated. Noah comes in again on Thursday. Aside from saying hello, though, there's not much interaction there. I don't *want* to be disappointed, but….

Look. I'm just gonna say it. Even if I'm not looking *for* anything, that doesn't mean he is not nice to, you know, look *at*. Can I not enjoy my view while I'm at work? Is that too objectifying of me? Maybe I shouldn't say it like that, but I think you get what I mean.

I otherwise have no windows because they're all in the counselor's offices. I'm right in the middle of the whole office at our front desk. I suppose I can look out into the hallway. The front wall of our office is all window, floor to ceiling.

Speaking of that large window wall, it is now Friday and Noah is standing outside talking to someone from another office. I know I shouldn't be staring, but he keeps smiling and oh my, God is it cute.

He's wearing a green shirt, a shirt that definitely brings out the color of his eyes and I'm sure he has to know that. He wore three different green shits this week. Does he do this to women on purpose, or does he just like how he looks in green? Maybe it's his favorite color.

Oh no! No… no no.

He caught me staring.

Great.

The conversation is ending. Whether because it was already going to, or because now he's decided to come here to find out why I'm staring at him, I don't know. And would you look at that? He is now coming this way. No no no I don't have a way to justify the staring.

Wait!

I could always say I was simply zoned out and happened to be looking in that general direction. Who's to say I was even looking directly at him? He can't prove that. I instinctively tense up when the door opens. Clearly, Sarah notices this as she lets out a quiet giggle.

"Hey, Noah!" she greets him cheerfully. "Something we can do for you?"

"Nah, I'm just stopping by. I figured I'd check in on Charlie here, make sure you guys haven't scared her away yet."

"Pfft. If anyone's gonna scare her away it's gonna be you."

"Ouch! That hurts. I am *not* a scary person. Am I?" he asks.

He turns to me and it takes me a moment longer than it should for me to realize I'm the one he's asking.

"Oh! Uh... no!"

He smiles, turns back to Sarah.

"See?"

She rolls her eyes.

"Charlie just doesn't know you well enough yet," she replies.

He laughs, feigns hurt.

"What did I do to you today, Sarah? I came in here to be a nice person and check on our new friend here and I gotta say, I'm feeling pretty attacked right now."

"Omg, you didn't just say that."

He laughs again.

"You guys do know I'm sitting right here?" I finally ask.

Noah looks at me and I sorta wish I'd kept my mouth shut, because his eyes are just too intense and now I feel like my face is starting to turn red and he probably notices. Oh, God! What if he figures it out? What if he can somehow read my mind and figures out that I've been thinking about him a little too much?

"Apologies. You are absolutely right and we are being rude. Well… Sarah's distracting me, so clearly it's just her being rude."

"Hey!" she says loudly.

"Anyway, how are you? I feel like I haven't asked that yet. Settling in fine? Like it here? Like all these weird, I mean *wonderful* people?"

"Uh… Yes."

He keeps staring. Clearly, he is expecting me to say more and I'm drawing a complete blank. I probably look stupid right now. He probably thinks there must not be much going on upstairs for me.

"Yes...?" he finally asks. "Is that to, like, all of the above, or...?"

"S-sorry, uh... yeah. Sorry. It's going well. I-I like it here a lot so far."

"Good, good. Glad to hear that." He opens his mouth as though to say something more and then closes it. Finally, he says, "I should probably get back to work and stop keeping you from yours."

"Yep. Bye!" Sarah calls out.

He only smiles, otherwise leaves without another word.

"You're kinda mean to him," I say once the door closes behind him.

She laughs.

"Don't let him fool you. He's usually a pain in the ass. He's only holding back because he doesn't know you well enough yet. Also, he probably *is* starting to think he may actually be scaring you off."

She lets out a laugh, but my heart sinks at the comment.

"What? Why? H-he's not!"

"Don't have to tell *me* twice."

"It's more likely he thinks I'm dense," I say. "He probably wonders how I even managed to get this job."

She sighs.

"No, that is most definitely not the case. I know him well enough to know that he probably thinks you're just shy and is worried he may come off as too strong of a personality. He's not judgmental. If anything, he's kind of a sensitive person."

I only have a moment to consider that before a new family walks through the door to check in for their tour. And then another. And another. Within minutes our lobby is full of people, and the sheer volume of noise is preventing me from being able to hear my own thoughts.

It stays busy like this all morning. I'm thankful for how quickly it makes time fly, as I'm starving. Before I know it, it's my lunch time. Since I'm new and don't know many people on campus I eat upstairs by myself.

There's a small seating area/lounge type space that I like to go to. I could leave campus, but my lunches are only half an hour in the summer and I've already learned that that barely gives you enough time to do literally anything.

So, instead I bring my own lunch from home and sit alone upstairs. It sounds pathetic, but I prefer the quiet. It's a welcome moment to relax, especially when we have a busier day. I'm sitting upstairs today like always.

Except today I am not alone. Not for long, anyway.

"Hey!"

I'm engrossed in my phone when I hear his voice. It startles me. I must look like a deer caught in headlights when I snap my head up to look at him. Noah is coming toward me and I realize he's going to sit next to me. Why did I sit on a bench? I don't know if I can handle being this close.

"Hi," I answer quietly.

"You don't mind if I join you, do you?" he asks. "It's okay if you do! I can go elsewhere."

"No. It's fine. You can."

He smiles and sits down. At max, he is two feet away from me.

My heart is hammering in my chest.

Chapter Four

There's this really awkward silence where neither of us say anything. I am way too self-aware of how I eat in that moment. Like, why did I not bring something small I could pick at or you know… not long noodles. I have parmesan garlic noodles with meatballs. I'd like to say I cooked, but the most I had to do was boil water and microwave frozen meat. Regardless, I can't eat this "nicely." I'm gonna look like a slob slurping up these noodles for sure.

"Has Sarah been filling your head with bad things about me yet?" he asks.

He doesn't look over at me, thankfully, because when he's not looking directly at me I can talk easier.

"Just that you can be annoying," I admit.

He laughs.

"Sounds about right."

"Why? Are there bad things to tell that I should be warned about?"

"No! No. Nothing like that. We just give each other a lot of shit. I like to warn new people that not everything she says is true. Although in this case I *am* kind of annoying, so I'll give her that."

I don't know what to say in response to that. My mind is drawing a blank. I would say he's not, but what do I know? I could assure him that I doubt he is. That's a more general thing to say, right? Why is this so hard? I'm not usually this shy. That's part of why I took this job. I love talking to and working with people. I can talk to total strangers with so much ease. But this man sitting next to me….

"Charlie?"

I realize he's been waiting for me to respond and I'm staring at the ground, not even eating at this point.

"Oh. Um. Sorry. I'm not usually this… spacey. I promise."

When I look up his eyes are on me again, except now I'm really close to him and can see all the different shades of green and they've somehow managed to become even prettier. And the freckles. I can definitely see that he has freckles now. Not sure how I missed that before. This man literally walked straight out of a Taylor Swift song.

"That's okay," he assures me. "You're new. You don't know me. I'm sure that annoying factor is kicking in by now since you can't seem to get rid of me. In fact, I *swear* I didn't follow you up here. I was coming up anyway." He pauses. "Am I right, though?"

I need to look away or I'm not going to be able to keep talking.

"The first two, yes," I say. "I don't think you're annoying, though."

I can see him smile out of the corner of my eye.

"Well, I'm glad. I'm not trying to be annoying in this case."

"In this case?"

"Well, yeah. Typically, I *am* trying."

I laugh at this, only slightly more relaxed than when he first sat down.

"Thanks for letting me know."

He leans back. I realize he's not actually eating anything and wonder what it was he originally came up for. Whatever it is, it must not be very important, because he's not getting up and leaving.

"Seriously, though. If you want me to leave you alone I will."

When I look over again he's staring up at the ceiling.

"Huh?"

"I realize I… I may be giving an unfavorable first impression of myself, like I'm some stalker. Or maybe I'm just paranoid. I don't know."

"No," I practically whisper. "I'm pretty sure that's me you're talking about with the unfavorable first impression. I'm not typically so absent minded or shy. It's just, this is all new for me. This job. You know, being an actual adult and all that. I care about it a lot more than

I have my previous jobs, so I don't want to fuck anything up. Unfortunately, I'm so worried about it that it's making me awkward and I mess things up and-"

"Hey," he cuts me off. "You've been here for a week. Don't be so hard on yourself. To put it bluntly, you're gonna fuck some shit up, but that's to be expected. Nobody learns these kinds of jobs in a week."

There's also the problem that my brain just ceases to function whenever he talks to me or looks at me, but I'm going to leave that part out.

"Thanks. I know that. I just have a hard time accepting it. It's... an issue of mine. One of many."

Not sure why I'm telling him *that*.

I realize he's looking at me again, but I don't have it in me to look back. I keep thinking he's going to comment on what I just said. He doesn't, though. He gets up instead.

"Well, I should let you eat your lunch in peace for the next," he looks at his watch, "five whole minutes! Sorry I took up so much of your time."

"Oh, no. It's okay."

He smiles, but he doesn't say anything more before turning and walking away. Did that conversation really just happen? Did he really just sit next to me? So close? The moment he's out of sight my brain is firing off a million questions and a million thoughts on the matter.

-

"You have to give me all of the details!" Sarah almost yells when I tell her about Noah and I eating lunch together.

I roll my eyes.

"I literally ate food and we talked. That is it. Nothing more."

"Boo. Boring."

I shake my head. Sometimes *she* can be a pain in ass. I'm not sure why she calls Noah one, because out of the two of them, he is way more chill. But like I said, I like Sarah. We get along great. We seem to work together really well too. I wouldn't trade her for a different coworker.

People mostly check in in the morning, so there aren't too many people to check in after lunch. While everyone is out on tour, the office is quiet for the first time today. I like the quiet today, though. As an introvert, I have to take time to get used to being around so many people every day. I worked in the back room at my last retail job, so there were five of us at most on any given day. Not too much interaction needed. This is pretty much the exact opposite of that.

Don't get me wrong. I absolutely love the excitement in the air being given off by prospective students and their families. The more people, the more excitement. Hearing people laugh, seeing them smile, seeing the relief in their eyes when they're helped with something they thought was going to be really difficult. The empath in me soaks it up like a sponge.

"What makes you assume I even want to date right now?" I ask. "I just got my own place not too long ago. I just started a new job. I'm kinda focusing on myself at the moment."

"You're thirty years old, you don't have a whole lot longer to focus on yourself if you want to get married and have kids," she replies.

"What if I don't?"

"Do you?"

I don't… know.

If I'm being completely honest, there are multiple reasons why I don't see a traditional life working out for me, and I'm not sure if it's even what I want to begin with. Maybe I'm taking too long to decide, but I don't feel like I fully have myself figured out, so how am I supposed to know what I want for my future that far down the road? Is this something I should have figured out by now?

It is true that most of the people I graduated high school with are married with children. They're becoming homeowners and buying cars that aren't almost as old as they are. If I were to compare myself to them, then yeah, I'm way behind. But life isn't a race, or so I've been told, so why does that even matter?

I realize I haven't answered her yet. She's staring at me, waiting, much like Noah had been. I need to pull myself together and force my brain to be a little more present.

"I haven't put much thought into it," I finally tell her. "I've always had more urgent matters at the forefront of my brain. The past several years have been a little hectic, to say the least. Even simple dating hasn't been a real concern of mine."

"Hectic how?"

I don't want to answer this. Not yet. I want to make sure people see the good side of me for as long as possible before the other side inevitably shows itself. I'm not going to tell her that I've been suffering with varying levels of depression and anxiety for half my life. Yeah. I've skated around that fact, but it's not like there's ever really a good time to tell someone about that kind of shit. And shit it is.

"Just… school, work, getting my own place for the first time. All that. I just want to be settled before I think about dating."

Oh, and also my biggest fear is that my crippling mental health issues will scare people away... scare Noah away. Obviously, though, I do not tell her this.

Everything Is Alright

Chapter Five

Since I've officially brought it up instead of casually trying to skirt around it for a little longer, I suppose I need to explain some things. Feeling like I'm not good enough for Noah, feeling like I won't fit in with the people I work with, worrying about living alone, there's a reason for all of that.

I first started struggling with my mental health when I was 14 years old. It's gotten easier to deal with since then, especially because I've been good at "mas-king" my symptoms, but I can't always. Things are still rough from time to time. It's not easy.

I know the logical option would probably be to go to therapy and I would if I could. We have a lack of mental health resources in our area, though. I've tried five different places and none of them are taking on new patients. There's a program here at work that I can use, but it only allows for my insurance to cover eight app-ointments a year. Kinda dumb if you ask me. I know I need something more regular than that.

For now, though, I'm going to act like everything is all fine and dandy. I'm going to convince my co-workers that I have my shit together like they all seem to, and I'm going to try and avoid the whole 'Noah being cute' thing. I didn't lie to Sarah. I really do want to settle in before I consider dating anyone, or even looking for that matter. I've already got a lot of work to do convincing people that I can handle my job and being on my own.

I revisit the idea of getting a cat when I return home for the day. An emotional support animal would be good for me, I think. I wouldn't feel so alone. I'd be more motivated to keep up my apartment so that my cat would be comfortable. I would never feel right bringing one home and letting it live in a mess. Perfect motivation.

I drop my bag and flop down on my bed, pulling out my phone and looking up local animal shelters. The closest one is about a 15-minute drive, but that's okay. I can easily do that on a weekend.

There are currently ten adoptable cats. I don't want a kitten, because I wouldn't feel safe leaving one home alone all day, but I do want a buddy that I'll have around for a while. Two to three years old seems perfect, and four of the cats fall into that age range. Let's see….

There's Mittens. Not very creative naming. Like all cats with that name, her paws look like mittens because they're all white in comparison to her mostly black body. Yeah, I'm that judgmental. She's cute, though.

Three years old. Would do well in a household with no other cats. Not a problem.

Dust Bunny. I'm not sure if that's cute or insulting to name your cat. He's a Russian Blue, though that means in color he's actually a very pretty, silvery gray. Two years old. Friendly and outgoing. Likes attention. Also doesn't do well with other cats.

Flower. Cute name I guess. I'd probably change it to something more suitable. She just doesn't look like a Flower. She's two years old and friendly. Shy at first and takes time to warm up to you. Not a bad thing. Understandable, really. She's a fluffy girl, and I've heard long-furred cats are actually better for people with allergies.

Last but not least we have Mason. Ginger kitty. Three years old. Playful. Not good with kids, but again, not an issue here. Does well with all other animals, though. Likes to be pet, but on his terms. Again, understandable. Ooh! Knows how to play fetch. That's pretty cool.

I fill out an interest form and set up a time this weekend to go visit the shelter. Then I make a note on my phone listing all the things I'll need to buy to be prepared for a cat. After that, I look around and realize there needs to be room for a litter box somewhere, and room isn't exactly something I have much of. Normally, my go-to would be the bathroom, but there is no way it's fitting in there.

There are litter box hiders that are designed to look like regular furniture. Maybe I can get one of those and put it out in my living room. I could put stuff on top since it can be used for a table as well. Nobody would know the difference. The only problem is they are *not* cheap. I consider that maybe I can squeeze the litter box somewhere in my bedroom, but then I just say fuck it and order the fancy one that looks like furniture.

My cat will get only the best. As long as I can afford it at least. Technically, this isn't my wisest financial decision, but the money is there. I just won't have a whole lot left. For now. But it's worth it, right? This cat is going to help me emotionally. I'm bettering myself. I go ahead and include the recommended litter box that will fit inside the whole contraption.

After a dinner of cereal and four episodes of the TV show I'm currently binging, it's time for bed. But when I lie down I'm unable to fall asleep, because there's just one thing from my day that I cannot get out of my head no matter how hard I try. Maybe trying is the problem.

Lunch with Noah.

Again, with those eyes of his.

Those beautiful, intimidating, mesmerizing eyes that make you feel like you're being interrogated, even if he has a smile on his face. I don't want to be thinking about him. He is not supposed to be the focus of this week. Yet I can still see his smile. Hear his laugh and the softness of his voice.

Son of a Bee. *Why*?

Sarah said he's single. Again… How? Nobody that looks like him should be single. Maybe that means there's something seriously wrong with him that drives women away. That's good. I'll just keep that in mind. Clearly a man as cute as him is not single because women are not interested. Sarah said it herself. Just about every woman in our office has a crush on him. Must be something about his personal life that nobody gets to see when he's at work.

Maybe he's a slob, or a hoarder, or both. Maybe he hates kittens and puppies and other cute little animals. Maybe he's a workaholic and doesn't have time for dating. Maybe he's picky, or expects women to take care of him. *Maybe* he doesn't tip when he eats out and he treats restaurant workers like crap, like they're beneath him.

To be honest, I can't see that last one being a real option, but who's to say for sure. It's possible the sweet, smiling, friendly act at work is just that, an act.

I need to keep my focus on where it should be, though, my job. I still have a lot to learn. I can't be distracted. I need to make a good impression so they don't feel like they've made a mistake hiring me. I still have a hard time seeing myself as an adult, and don't need my behavior reflecting that. I already have a face that makes me look at least ten years younger than I actually am. In fact, I do still get mistaken for a student all the time. There's also the fact that I feel so unsure of myself. I'd like to say I'm a confident person, but that would be lying.

The thing is, I've spent too much of my life only ever being told what I did wrong. Even when I've accomplished things I've been proud of, it seems like those things were always dulled in comparison to what *hadn't* gone right. It's made it so that I've stopped focusing enough on the good things and only seem to focus on the bad. And even though I know that about myself, it doesn't mean it's been any easier to get out of that bad habit.

All of these things are running through my mind. I've fallen down a rabbit hole and I'm falling faster and faster the farther I get.

All because of a guy.

How is it possible that he already has this much of an effect on me? What is it about him? Something's different. I know that much. Typically, it takes me a while to warm up to someone, and I don't usually notice people unless they make an effort. Like, I need to get to know someone as a friend first, or I'm not even gonna give them a second glance. That's how I've always been.

Maybe I'm worrying too much about this. Maybe it's nothing. Maybe I just think he's cute and that's it and I am blowing this out of proportion in my own mind because clearly, I'm already stressed about starting a new job. That's gotta be it, right? Like, I'm just looking for something to go wrong. I'm looking for a reason to chicken out and say I can't do this.

Right?

Everything Is Alright

Chapter Six

I've done my best to clear my mind before the next morning. New day. Fresh start. Let's just focus on what I need to be focused on. I get to go visit the animal shelter today and hopefully take a kitty home. I'm hoping Dust Bunny is still there. He seems like the best choice, granted he doesn't hate me I suppose. There is that to consider. Not just for me, but I wouldn't want to make him stressed out all the time if he doesn't like being around me.

They say you don't choose the cat, the cat chooses you, so I hope he likes me. I'm not opposed to taking home another cat. I just feel a vibe from him. That probably sounds stupid. I know.

I do a little shopping in the morning since the shelter doesn't open until noon. I kind of go overboard on the toys, but it's just so much fun and everything is so cute.

When I finally arrive at the shelter, the woman at the front desk greets me.

"You must be Charlie!" she says cheerfully.

"Hi. Yeah. That would be me."

"Awesome! Just follow me."

I follow her farther into the shelter and around a corner to the left. We enter a room with a wall of kennels, some of which have cats in them. There are a few different ones from when I looked online, but I do see that Dust Bunny is still here.

"Can I take them out?" I ask.

"Of course! I'll just shut the door."

Some of the cats back away, hiding in the corners of their cages and it makes me feel sad for them. Some of them meow at me. Some try to reach out with their paws. Actually… all of them kind of make me sad, because I can't take every cat home with me, but all of them deserve a loving home.

Dust Bunny is one of the cats to come forward and meow at me. He sticks his little nose to the cage door to try and sniff me and I scratch his head by sticking a finger through the bars.

"Hey, buddy," I say.

I open the cage door and he hops right out, circling me and rubbing up against my legs. When I sit down on the floor, he climbs into my lap and rubs against my chest, bumping my chin with the top of his head.

"He's very affectionate," the woman tells me. "We're pretty sure he loves everyone, so I don't think you two would have any trouble getting along."

I let out a giggle as he spins around excitedly and his tail hits my face. He very much enjoys being pet.

"I can see that," I reply. "He's so cute!"

The woman smiles.

"He's one of the ones that's been here a bit longer. He's still young, but I'm sure you know how so many people want a kitten instead of a fully-grown cat."

I nod.

"I can see that. He would be perfect for me, though. I don't think I'd be ready to take care of a little kitten, especially since I wouldn't feel safe leaving one home alone while I work. My mom had a cat who was ten years old and still got into things all the time, but I still feel kittens require quite a bit of extra work."

"They do," she agrees. "That's one of the issues we have here. We get so many kittens returned all the time, because someone's kid thought they wanted one, but then they bring them back saying it's a bigger responsibility than the kid expected and the parents just don't have the time for it. Or it grew up and it's not cute enough anymore."

"That's really sad."

"It is, and it's really hard on us, because we can't exactly say no to someone on the grounds that we 'assume' they'll end up bringing the cat back. We try to screen potential adopters as best as we can, but… it's not always easy."

"That makes sense." Dust Bunny sits down in my lap and starts purring contentedly. I look at the other cats in their cages. “I wish I could help them all find good homes,” I tell her. “It’s unfortunate I can only take one.”

Flower and Mittens are still here amongst the new arrivals. Mason is gone. Someone was probably really excited to adopt a cat that could play fetch.

“You have to have a tough heart to be able to work in a place like this. I will say that. Can’t let it get you down that you can’t guarantee a forever home for all of them.”

“I can see that too.” Dust Bunny leans into me, almost like he’s giving me a little hug. “I think I was right about this one, though. I sort of had a feeling he’d be a good fit for me, and it seems like he agrees.”

“Great! There’s some more paperwork we need you to fill out if you’d like to adopt him, and some things we can send you home with. Dusty has been here a while and a very kind couple gave us some things to send home with him to hopefully entice people to take him into consideration more. Just follow me back out to the front desk.”

As I follow her out, carrying Dust Bunny in my arms so they can put him into his carrier, there’s another family coming in and another worker bringing them to where they keep the dogs. The already loud barking intensifies as they walk through the door.

A girl who I assume to be one of the volunteers comes and puts the carrier on the counter for Dust Bunny. He isn’t too thrilled about being moved to a much smaller space, so I try to assure him that it's only for a little while, even though I know he doesn't understand me. He pushes his head against the top and paws at it. Then the meowing begins.

They give me a small amount of the food they've been feeding him to get me started, a couple toys, and a small bag of litter. I load it all up in my car. He's curled up now, no longer pawing at the door, but he is still meowing.

"I promise. You'll be home soon."

-

I've changed his name to Dusty. The other name felt too weird. When we get back to my apartment I make sure to close the door tight and then let him out of his carrier. I've already set up a small cat tree for him, and I have the few toys they gave me plus the ones I've already bought. I also got him a really nice fluffy bed. He comes out slowly, sniffing the air.

"This is your new home," I tell him. "I hope you like it."

The first thing he does is crawl underneath my couch. I think he's gonna hide for a while, but he comes out after a minute or two. He walks in a crouched down position, but he does walk around.

I'm glad to see that he's not totally afraid to explore his new surroundings. It's cute how he will put his front paws up on my chair to get a better look, and then go peek around the corner of my bedroom door before going in and checking out my bed. I have a feeling he's not going to sleep in *his* too often.

After showering, changing into pajamas, cooking and eating dinner, and then cleaning up the dishes, I relax on my couch and watch a movie. I'm about halfway through when Dusty comes and jumps up onto the couch. He doesn't crawl into my lap like earlier, though. Instead, he curls up next to my leg for a nap. Maybe he already knows this is his forever home.

"I think you're going to help me out a lot, Dusty. It already feels better with you here. I know you can't talk back, nor can you understand me, but just having you here next to me is nice."

I pet him and he starts purring, though his eyes stay closed.

"Seems like you enjoy being here with me too. I bet it was lonely in that shelter. I'll make sure you don't feel too alone while I'm gone at work all day. I wish I could bring you with, but I'm pretty sure our office has a "no pet" policy."

His eyes may be closed, but his ears twitch while I talk, so I know he's not fully asleep.

I wonder if Noah likes cats.

Wait. Why does that matter? I am *not* thinking about bringing him home with me. He has no reason to meet Dusty. I mean I know you can invite friends over casually and not have anything inappropriate happen, but still. It is way too soon to be thinking about that. I haven't even considered going anywhere off campus with him. Hell, we haven't even left our building to go anywhere else *on* campus.

Nope. I need to slow down. Way down. I need to all but come to a complete stop before I start putting other ideas in my head. Like… how would it feel to have such an attractive guy sitting on my couch so close to me, even if we're just friends? What if it were to make me want him closer to me? I know we've sat on a bench together, but that is *not* the same thing. That is in public. This is in my own private space. Just the two of us. Alone.

It's… not a bad thought.

Everything Is Alright

Chapter Seven

I hate thinking things about people that I shouldn't be thinking, because then my paranoid ass sits here all day and worries that maybe they'll know, that maybe they can read my mind. I know that's ridiculous, and I know that people can't read my mind. I shouldn't be worrying that Noah will somehow inherently know that I had been imagining him in my apartment. He won't know that for a brief moment I pictured the two of us cuddled up on my couch together. Yet here I am.

It's not helping me be less nervous.

When he stops in our office on Monday I almost don't want to look at him. I do, though. It would be rude to ignore him. Might also look a little suspicious.

"Hey," he says with a smile.

"Hi," I respond quietly.

"How's it goin' so far today?" he asks.

I shrug.

"Okay, I guess. We're gonna get pretty busy today. Seems to be the trend for Mondays and Fridays. I like it. Makes the day go by fast. Or feel like it, I guess I should say."

"What do you want now, Noah?" Sarah cuts in.

What the hell, Sarah?

Noah hands her a piece of paper like he usually does.

"Got another one for you to look up. So," he says, turning back to me. "Lunch today?"

I can see Sarah's big grin from the corner of my eye.

"Yeah. That sounds good."

"Cool." He stands patiently waiting, quiet. "I think a few of your visitors actually have appointments with me today," he finally says.

My heart is hammering away in my chest. As he's looking at me, clearly waiting for me to respond in some way, the Noah in my head has an arm around me and I'm leaning against him. I don't notice that I'm actually staring at him until Sarah clears her throat next to me.

Crap.

"Uh… sorry. I'm just tired. I believe you're right, though. Don't scare them away, now."

I smile so he knows that I'm joking and am rewarded with a smile in return.

"I promise I'll be on my best behavior."

"Not fair!" We both turn to Sarah. "You're never on your best behavior for *me*," she complains. "You always say you'll purposely scare them away and *blame* it on me."

He laughs.

"What? No. I'm pretty sure I've never said that." He looks at me. "Don't listen to her," he tells me. "She doesn't know what she's talking about."

"Oh, get outta here, Noah. You liar."

He doesn't say anything more as she hands him the paper back and gives him his answer. Instead he smiles at me and then turns to walk out. As the door shuts, Erik comes around the corner and leans on the side of Sarah's desk.

"You really should be nicer to Noah," he says. "He's going to start sending someone else in his place."

Sarah laughs out loud.

"First of all," she says, "You have a husband. You don't need to be checkin' him out. Second, I'm pretty sure I could start being even more mean to him and he would still show up to see Charlie."

"Wha- No!" I practically yell. "What have I told you, like, a hundred times?"

She turns to Erik instead of answering me.

"Charlie says she just wants to be friends with him and that he clearly doesn't look at her that way. I say bull, because he's so much more smiley now that Charlie's here."

Erik raises his eyebrows, clearly surprised.

"I was starting to think nobody had a chance with that man."

Everything Is Alright

I'm starting to think everyone in this office cares more about my love life than they do my work ethic. They care about my love life more than *I* care about my love life. And it's *my* love life… or lack thereof.

The minutes somehow fly by. It's nearing my lunch time now, and I'm getting nervous. I have to sit with him? I have to talk to him? After last night? What if I let something slip? It's possible. I sometimes say stupid shit when I get nervous. I can't even imagine how he would react.

I also already know I'm going to get bombarded with questions when I get back from lunch. Why did he have to ask in front of people? Does he not know what assumptions people are making? Does he know and just not care what people think? Maybe I'm overthinking this. I overthink things easily.

He's waiting for me outside my office when I walk out the door, leaning up against the wall. I'd say he's not a full foot taller than me, but close. A good height for me. He smiles when he looks over at me.

"Hey," he says.

"Hi."

We walk upstairs together. He's wearing a dark green, button down shirt with the sleeves rolled halfway up. Has he done this on purpose? He must know how well this shirt brings out the green in his eyes. He could melt any girl's heart with this combination.

Sitting this close to him, they *are* melting mine. I want to forget about my lunch altogether and just stare into his eyes the whole time, but since that would be creepy, I don't. I only steal glances when he looks my way.

"I got a cat," I say when I can't take any more silence.

Usually I don't mind it too much, but after last night… It's a good thing cuddling was all we did in my head, or I'd be a wreck right now. Probably wouldn't have even come into work.

Okay, that's a lie. I still would have. Obviously.

"Oh, cool. Boy? Girl? Name? Cute?"

I laugh.

"Boy. Dusty. And he is the cutest."

Noah raises an eyebrow.

"I feel like all pet owners say that. How do I know you're telling the truth? Do you have a picture?"

"Err… sadly I don't."

He fake scoffs.

"Who gets a cat and isn't immediately taking one-hundred pictures to share with friends and post online? I will require that you bring cute cat pictures tomorrow, or we can't do lunch."

"Pfft. Whatever. I'll take pictures then. Do you have any pets?"

It doesn't slip past me that we just confirmed we both wanted to have lunch again tomorrow. Will this be a regular thing?

"Sadly no. I always had them growing up, but then I couldn't while I was in college and somehow I just haven't had it in me to go adopt one since then. I guess it's because I feel like I'm too busy most of the time."

"That's why you get a cat," I suggest. "Typically speaking, they can take care of themselves pretty well."

He thinks about this for a moment. It's kind of cute watching him sort of squint in concentration as he considers what I've said, as though it is a very important thing to consider.

"True," he finally says. "Orrrr, you could bring your cat here as an office therapy cat and I can just come visit."

"Nope. No can do. He's meant to keep me company at home. That's where he needs to be. Plus, as nice as our director is, I'm not sure he'd let us keep a cat in the office. Once it took a shit or something he'd say its gotta go."

He laughs.

"Fair point. Wouldn't want our Admissions office smelling like a litter box, especially if kitty had an upset stomach."

"Exactly."

I realize we're talking about cats shitting in the middle of eating lunch. It's a good thing we're just friends and this isn't a date. I'd totally be bombing it right now. You can't get much less sexy than this.

Of course, Noah doesn't seem to mind talking about such a topic right now. Maybe he's just kinda weird and that would be a perfectly acceptable topic even if this was a date. How should I know?

He sets his food container on the seat between us and stretches out, leaning all the way back with his legs straight out. He turns his head to look at me and it is so cute, especially when I can tell he's smiling, even out of the corner of my eye.

"What?" I ask, turning to look at him.

That's a mistake.

Cuteness overload.

He's still smiling.

"Nothing."

"It's not nothing," I argue. "You're looking at me like you're thinking something funny about me."

"You just have a small feather in your hair in the back."

"What? And you were considering *not* telling me?"

I'm going to reach back and try to find it, but he beats me to it. His hand brushes against mine. It's the slightest touch, but I can still feel it. When he gets it out he hands it to me.

"I thought maybe it could be a new hair accessory. You could've been a trend setter."

"Right."

I can see why it wasn't noticeable to my coworkers. It's almost the same color as my hair. He likely only noticed because he's so close to me. I want to say more, but I can't, because I can still feel his light touch, his fingers brushing against mine as he gently plucked it out of my hair.

I am dying on the inside.

Chapter Eight

The feather is from one of the toys I bought Dusty. I'm not sure how or when it made its way into my hair, but I can't put it down when I get back to the office. I just keep twirling it around in my fingers. How am I supposed to be Noah's friend? I can't be his friend if I'm going to feel like he's lighting a fire inside of my body every time he so much as brushes up against me even slightly. I didn't realize it was going to be this hard to ignore how clearly attracted to him I am.

"You okay?" Sarah asks. "What's that?"

She's pointing at the feather in my hand, which I've admittedly been staring at for longer than necessary.

"Oh. This is just a feather that came off a cat toy I bought. I found it in my hair earlier. I guess I just zoned out for a minute, but I'm fine. I promise."

She looks at me skeptically. It's like she knows I'm leaving something out.

"Okay. If you're sure."

I nod and smile. When she turns away, I stick the feather in the drawer underneath my desk. I can't get myself to throw it away just yet, but I don't want her to see that. Before I shut the drawer, I look at it again. It's a pastel teal, only slightly more blue than my mint green hair. The moment my eyes land on it again I go back to when we were sitting on that bench, the exact moment he reaches over to pluck it out for me.

Except in my head he doesn't just remove the feather. He rests his hand at the back of my neck, letting my hair spill over, and pulls me closer to him. I want to let my imagination run with this. I know he'll kiss me if I do.

But I shake my head.

No.

I can't.

I shut the drawer with a sigh and get back to my job. I'm currently not doing anything particularly useful and I feel like I can't sit still, so I tell Sarah I'm going to run and check the mail. She hands me the key to our mailbox and I leave the office. I've learned I like checking the mail or bringing it down simply to have a break from sitting for so long.

Plus, it's quiet in our building. Outside of my office that is. Since all of the offices are administrative, there's not usually a whole lot of excitement going on. I think working in one of the academic buildings would be too much for me.

In this quiet space I find my thoughts drifting back to Noah again. I mean… he is cute. He's nice, from what I've seen so far. Sarah thinks he's still single.

What if, and this is a hard what if… what if I *was* interested in being more than his friend? Sarah also seems to think he likes me. She could just be overly hopeful, though, and I'm not the kind of person to make a move unless I know for sure that my odds are good. In this case, I have absolutely zero clues to go by. Maybe I need to find a way to throw some hints out. See how he responds.

But that's only IF I decide this is something I would want to do. I know I keep telling myself that I did not start this job with hopes to find a man, but what if, maybe, it just happened that way? These things are possible.

We only have a small handful of what looks like high school transcripts in the mail. It'll be a quick job to sort and hand them to the appropriate processors. I was hoping for more, more of a distraction.

Once I get back, I sit down at my desk and immediately turn to Sarah.

What the hell. Just gonna go right ahead and throw it out there even though I already know what response I'm about to receive. Why not?

"What if… *hypothetically speaking*… I did want to be more than friends with Noah?"

"OH, MY GOD!" Sarah looks around, and apologizes to everyone who turned to look for the small outburst. "Seriously?" she says much quieter.

I shrug.

"I don't know, honestly. I really don't. The feather I was holding earlier, I lied about it. I didn't find it. He did, and he pulled it out for me and his hand touched me just a little bit and I'd be lying again if I said I didn't instinctively wish for more than just that small, half second moment of contact. So there. I've admitted it. I just… I don't want to upset him if he's just hoping for a friend. He probably gets women hitting on him all the time."

Clearly, he's single for a reason. What if it's simply because he wants to be?

Sarah contemplates what I've said for a moment. She thinks long and hard. I'm left awkwardly staring at her in the meantime, anxious about what she might respond with. Anxious about the fact that I just admitted that I like him.

"You know… he's always come to our office for things, but he's been coming around a little more often lately, even just for small things. If he thinks he doesn't want more than friendship he is in denial. You're not always looking, but I've noticed the brief smile when he sees that you're at your desk. He's happy you're not off doing something else, because that means he gets to see you."

My heart flutters in my chest. Does he really smile when he sees me at my desk?

"So, what do I do?"

"We can start small," she tells me. "I want you to look extra cute tomorrow. Dress like you're going on a date. Put on makeup. Fix your hair. Make yourself irresistible to be precise. But, you know, also work appropriate, obviously."

"I may need your help with that. I'll send you some pics of outfits I have when I get home."

"Awesome! If it makes him more awkward in the least bit, then he probably likes you and is trying to hide it. It'll be a noticeable difference to how he typically acts. At least, in most cases that's how I've seen guys respond. It's not a one-hundred percent guarantee."

-

When I get home, I go through literally every article of clothing I own, making a complete mess of my bedroom in the process. I pick out a few cute shirt and skirt options as well as a few dresses. Most of these things are pretty form fitting and, belly issue aside, I would like to think I have a pretty good figure. I'm willing to show that off a little.

Then there are shoes. I own like… seventy pairs of shoes. Why in the world do I have so many pairs of shoes? No wonder I was always going broke before. Pretty sure I just found the reason why.

I send pictures to Sarah of basically every pair. It takes her awhile to go through it all before I finally get a response back.

Sarah: `I think outfit #7 with shoe #4`

Me: `Thanks. I think you're right.`

Sarah: `The colors contrast enough, but still go together in a way that I think will go well with your hair.`

Outfit set. Pretty silver necklace picked out. I just have to get up a little earlier to curl my hair a bit and put on some cute, but still natural looking, makeup. I don't want to go too overboard, or he's gonna notice in a bad way. I don't want it to be obvious that I'm trying to get his attention.

When I go to bed that night I have a hard time falling asleep. Must be my nerves. I'm too busy thinking about tomorrow and if he'll actually even notice me dressing up a little more. Let's be honest. Some men are not good at noticing these things. It could go straight over his head and then I'll feel kind of dumb for bothering in the first place. I'm not even entirely sure why I've actually agreed to do this. It feels like there's no going back now, though. Sarah knows that I'm interested in him and something tells me she won't give up until the two of us are together.

I wonder if he'll even say anything if he does notice.

Will all of this effort be worth it?

I'm still awake late into the night.

Everything Is Alright

Chapter Nine

The next morning I do my hair and makeup, get dressed, and then take a look at myself in the mirror. Sarah and I picked out a sapphire blue shirt with short, ruffled sleeves and a flowy, white skirt that lands just above my knees. The skirt is accented with flowers that are the same shade of blue as my shirt. Also, for the first time in a while now, I am wearing heels. They're small heels, but still. Sarah told me they'd make my legs look longer, and since I'm only five feet tall I figured it would be worth it.

I put my necklace on, check my hair and face one more time, and head out.

Since there are days where Noah doesn't need to come to our office for anything, Sarah makes a call to the Financial Aid office and finds an excuse for him to come "help her with an incoming student." I'm not sure if they buy it or not, but either way, they send him over.

I'm not at my desk right now, but I am where I can see him, and Sarah predicted it correctly. There's a hint of disappointment in his expression when he looks where I should be sitting. I let her do her "work" related thing, trying to take deep breaths. When it seems like they're done talking and he's about to leave, I walk out from where I've been standing around the corner in our mail room.

And he lights up a little when he looks up and sees me. It's quick, but it's there.

"Hi," he says as I walk back to my spot.

It does not go unnoticed that he looks me over as I walk.

"Hey."

For once I think he doesn't know exactly what to say. I can practically see his mind trying to piece something together really quick.

"Anything in particular you uh… have… going on today? You seem a tad more dressed up than usual."

My heart is beating so fast I'm afraid I'm gonna go into cardiac arrest if it doesn't slow down soon.

"Oh. No," I respond awkwardly. "I just felt like putting a little more effort in. Sometimes a girl just wants to feel a little prettier, ya know?"

"Gotcha… well you do… look pretty, that is. Not that you typically don't! You just… you look nice. That's all. Sooooo, Sarah!" he turns back to her. "Everything good then? All sorted out?"

"Yep. All good!" she tells him.

"Great… great. I will see you all later then."

He gives a small wave as he walks out. Once he's gone, Sarah immediately turns to me.

"See? I told you!"

Some of the others in the office come out of their smaller, separated offices. Alice and Lydia come up front. Erik follows shortly after.

"Did I just hear what I think I heard?" Alice asks.

"Someone sounded a little flustered," Lydia adds. "Did we actually manage to find someone he might consider dating?"

My cheeks burn. I'm not a fan of having a lot of attention focused on me. I sort of just shrink into my desk space while everyone starts talking. Sarah notices and leans closer to me.

"Sorry for the extreme reaction," she says. "It may not seem like a big deal, but most of us just want him to be happy. As chipper as he may always seem, a few of us have noticed from time to time that there's a part of himself he tries to hide from us that slips out every so often. He's been alone for a long time."

I still do wonder *why*. Or *how*.

-

Today is another busier day, so once it gets going, it rarely stops. We have a lot of people checking in for tours, the phone is ringing more than usual, and some of the parents have questions that I do not know how to answer yet. It's a smidge stressful, to say the least, but somehow I'm still managing to stay on top of it all. Aside from our fifteen-minute breaks we're allowed, Sarah and I always have something to be doing or someone to be talking to.

This is closer to what it normally feels like in the office according to her. Of course, there are days when they've had twice as many visitors. She warns me that some days there will be so many people it's hard to fit them in our office. I sort of look forward to it for some weird reason. I like to be busy, even if I don't quite know what I'm doing yet.

Of course, I've also been told that I never will. Not one-hundred percent, anyway. Things are always changing and new, weird situations come up from time to time that even some of the people who have been here for years have never experienced. In a sense, you walk in every morning never fully knowing what to expect. A part of me kind of likes that about this job.

After running between offices to make sure our counselors know that their visitors have arrived, sorting a fairly large amount of mail and answering the phone all morning, it is finally time for me to go to lunch. I grab my food out of our mini fridge and practically run upstairs. Noah isn't waiting outside of our office today, nor is he upstairs, which makes me a little sad. Is he not coming? Has he figured it out and it scared him away?

I sit in the same spot as always, the bench that we've been sharing, and pull out my phone. With nothing else to do but scroll through various social media apps, I eat my lunch and wait. I really hope he shows up. And soon, since I only have half an hour.

I'm watching a "fail compilation" video when I hear footsteps quickly making their way up the stairs. When I look up, Noah is clearly slightly out of breath, but trying to hide it.

"Hey," he struggles to try and say casually. "Sorry I'm late."

He sits down and I'm almost certain he's sitting closer to me than usual.

"It's okay," I assure him. "I know your office is pretty much as busy as ours lately."

I am not sure what else to say, so I hold out my phone for him.

"What's this?" he asks.

"A stupid video if you want some entertainment while you eat."

He smiles.

"Okay. Here." He scoots over so that he is sitting right up against me. "So you don't have to hold it out so far."

Smooth, Noah. Smooth.

I look up from my phone and realize he's already looking at *me*. We are so close together. I do the only logical thing, clearly, and quickly look back to my phone and hit play on the next video. Out of the corner of my eye I can see him keep looking at me for a moment longer before he joins me in watching the video.

All I need to do is keep my breathing steady so that he doesn't notice just how nervous I actually am. Dammit. I'm the one who dressed up all cute and put extra effort into getting ready specifically to draw his attention and now that I have it I'm freaking out. Why is this not easier? Is it simply because I feel like men as cute as Noah don't usually look at me the way he seems to be? I don't know. It's not like I haven't been around other men before, though. I did mention my previous boyfriends after all.

It could also be because I'm used to men being a little more forward, but Noah is clearly on the hesitant side. It's cute actually. But also, I'm really bad at initiating things and so this is a little more difficult than what I would typically like.

"Your hair suits you, by the way." Noah is looking at me again when I glance up. "I don't think I've ever mentioned that, but I like the color. You really have to be able to pull that off, and not a lot of people can."

"Oh… thank you."

I want to kiss him. I *really* want to kiss him right now. I could. I feel like this is one of those moments where that would be acceptable. Then again, we're at work. Would that make it weird? I feel like a first kiss with someone shouldn't be while you're both at work, but that would mean I'd have to find a way to go somewhere else with him.

As I watch the minutes pass on my phone I realize I'm going to have to go back to work soon. Noah notices as well. I watch as he throws away trash and picks up the container he brought his lunch in. I'm going to have to be bold or he's going to just leave and....

"A few people from my office asked if I wanted to go out with them tonight. Just for a little bit. Drink or two. You can come with us if y-you want... they uh... said I could bring a friend if I wanted and I mean... they know you already... so I uh... I figured-"

"Sure."

"Great! Cool... um... I'll update you with details in a bit then... I don't know if you want to just come back over to our office or something..."

He smiles.

"Can I see your phone?"

"Huh? Oh. Yeah."

I hand him my phone and watch as he goes to my contacts and adds his number.

"You can just text me," he says as he hands it back.

Oh. My. God

Everything Is Alright

Chapter Ten

"You guys have to help me!" I shout as I walk back into our, thankfully empty at the moment, office. I can't believe I just did what I did.

"What's up?" Sarah asks.

"So… I kind of just told Noah that a few of us were going out for a bit tonight, because I was too afraid to ask him out with just me in case that made him uncomfortable or something and I thought maybe I'd just make it a more casual friend thing and, you know, see where that goes and now I need people to go out with so that he doesn't find out I technically lied about it."

I'm out of breath by the time I get that all out.

"No way! I mean yes! We can totally do that. But like… no way! I can't believe you technically sort of asked him out. I will rally a team!"

I laugh.

"I can't either. Sounds good, though. Thank you so much!"

Sarah manages to get Alice, Lydia, two counselors I can't say I've talked to much, and Erik, who will be bringing his husband with him, because his husband always shows up in our office at the end of the day to pick him up anyway.

Thank all of the Gods and Goddesses of all the religions! It would have been so embarrassing if I had to admit it would just be the two of us.

Anyway, we've picked a bar to go to for a quick drink. At the end of the day we agree that we'll meet each other there. I've already texted Noah to fill him in, to which I get the reply:

`Noah: Okay! :)`

His seemingly genuine excitement has me smiling from ear to ear.

I head to the bar and when I climb out of my car, he's already there, waiting by the door. Alice and Lydia arrive together, immediately after us. We talk as we wait for the others and, once everyone has arrived, head in together. We grab a table near the back and sit down.

Noah sits next to me and leans back in his chair. It's fun talking outside of work where we can all say whatever we want. It's also nice to formally meet Jeff, Erik's husband. He's a pretty chill guy. A little on the quieter side, which is the complete opposite of Erik.

Noah also doesn't seem to mind that he's the only one who works in a different office, but I suppose it helps that they all know each other already. I'm really the only odd one out. I notice Noah keeps looking over at me and every so often checking in to make sure that I'm comfortable as, admittedly, I am not talking a whole lot here.

I'm just not good at jumping into conversations where a lot of people are talking. I'm more of a wait-until-it-gets-quiet-again type person.

"You want to step outside for a bit?"

I look up from where I'd been staring at the drink in my hand to see Noah waiting for an answer.

"Yeah. Sure."

Sarah gives me a quick wink when Noah tells everyone we'll be right back.

Once outside, I realize it's gotten a little chillier out. Even though it's summer, it's easy to see that fall will be coming along quickly.

"This isn't really your kind of thing, is it?" he asks when we're alone.

I shake my head.

"Never been one for bars, but… I denied them once already so I figured I'd give it a shot." That's totally a lie, but whatever. "I'm glad I invited you, though. I don't think I'd feel comfortable enough on my own."

He smiles.

"I'm glad you invited me too."

He starts unbuttoning his shirt.

"Uh… what are you doing? Aren't you going to get cold?" I ask. "It's actually a little chilly right now for a summer evening, and-"

"I know." He takes the shirt off and drapes it over my shoulders, true gentleman style. "But *you* looked like you were getting a little cold. I'll be fine."

He's wearing a plain, white t-shirt and somehow making it look really good in a way I don't think most people could. I mean, it's a plain, white t-shirt. Oh, and his shirt smells like him and it's a really nice, soft, clean smell like freshly done laundry. I put my arms through the sleeves that are too long for me. Noah chuckles at my side.

"What?" I ask, glancing up at him.

"Nothing. You just… you're so small."

I roll my eyes.

"Yeah. I'm aware of that."

He looks down at me, those green eyes of his making my knees weak.

"It's cute. That's all."

He looks away, out at the street. It's obvious he's a little nervous right now. So am I. We're alone. Sort of. And we're outside of work. Sadly, I don't have it in me to say or do anything more. We stand in silence for a moment, watching the cars drive by. I've wrapped his shirt tightly around me. Honestly, I don't want to take it off and give it back to him.

"It's kinda nice getting out and getting some fresh air," he says after a while. "The overwhelming smell of alcohol mixed with cigarette smoke can be a little too much after a while."

"Yeah. I agree."

He takes a deep breath, lets it out slowly.

"On that note, though, we should probably head back inside," he suggests. "You know, before they all think we ditched them."

Right. We should.

I feel like he gave me an opportunity by coming out here and I'm blowing it by being a chicken.

He turns to walk back inside, but I can't just let him go. I can't.

"Noah."

He turns back to me.

I don't really think. I just act. If I think I chicken out. If I think I give myself time to imagine the outcomes and let's just say I'm not the optimistic type.

So, I don't think.

I just do.

I stand on the tips of my toes, put my hands around his neck, and pull him into a kiss. Unsurprisingly, he is caught off guard. His whole body goes tense for a short moment, but eventually I feel his hands on my waist, and not to push me away, thankfully. He holds onto me as he kisses me back. This close, I can feel that *my* heart isn't the only one racing.

I pull back.

"I… I'm sorry if-"

"Don't be."

"You sure?"

He smiles.

"I like you, Charlie."

Oh. My. God.

"You don't know me," I say.

Why did I just say that?

Why the hell couldn't I just tell him I liked him too?

"I'd like to," he answers without skipping a beat.

I don't know how to respond to that. My grade A awkwardness is sneaking in to ruin the moment. He pulls me into a hug and holds me for a moment, and in that moment, everything feels… good. He asks if it's okay.

"Yes! Definitely!" I spit out just a *hair* too enthusiastically.

Then we remember we were about to go back inside, so that's what we do.

Everyone else at the table seems to be having a great time. Sarah, seeing us first, announces to everyone that we've come back. Shit. I'm still wearing his shirt. I start to take it off to give back to him, but he stops me.

"Keep it for now. You don't have a jacket with you."

"Has it finally happened?" Erik asks. "Are you two a thing yet?"

"Oh, my God!" Sarah calls out. "Erik, you can't just ask that!"

"Why not? Everyone here wants to know. Y'all just aren't brave enough."

"Isn't that why we're here?" Alice asks.

Sarah nudges her.

"Alice!"

No. Please. Please do not tell him the truth.

"What?" Alice turns to Noah and I know I'm done for. "Charlie was too afraid to ask you on an actual date, so here we are. Not that we don't want to hang out with you guys. Obviously."

Oh boy.

I expect him to get mad or something. Confused at the least. Instead, when I look over, I see he's smiling at me.

"Oh, really?" he asks.

I want to crawl under the table right now. This is too much. Too soon. I should have thought this through more. Of course they'd blab and tell him. I want to shrink away until I feel his hand on mine. The smile on his face as he looks at me makes my cheeks burn like never before.

"Maybe," I admit.

He laughs, but not a mean laugh. He's not laughing *at* me.

"I guess I can be the one to ask you on our first *official* date then," he tells me.

Queue cheers from everyone around us. Noah turns completely red and hides his face, which is about as adorable as it gets.

"We've only been trying to find him a girl for a while now," Lydia tells me.

His face is still red. He doesn't seem to like a lot of attention on him either. It's so cute.

"It's true," he tells me. "They really have been. Don't think I didn't see the look you gave me when I walked in on Charlie's first day, *Sarah*."

He shoots *her* a look.

"What? Me? A look? You must be mistaken."

We keep talking. Keep laughing. I feel more relaxed now, though it might be because Noah's arm is around me. I am very comfortable here. It's about time I admit to myself that, yes, I can get a new job and a boyfriend at the same time and not completely fall apart.

-

I fall into bed that night, scaring Dusty, who had previously been sound asleep. With a quick apology and some pets, he forgives me and curls up at my side. I'm still wearing Noah's shirt. I didn't take it off when I came inside. I don't want to. Dusty gives it a good sniff before deciding that it's not anything important.

Chapter Eleven

Normally, I wouldn't want to walk to work, because I don't want to end up sweaty, but the weather's really nice today and I'm in a really good mood. I'll just wear a tank top and put a cardigan over it when I get to work. Bam! Instantly professional. Less likely to be smelly and gross when I get there. I'll also make a note to get some deodorant to keep in my desk.

It's actually very nice to walk by myself. Peaceful, I'd say. Because it's early in the morning, there's barely any traffic. We're in a small town, though, so it's not like there would be a whole lot regardless, I suppose.

There are workers cutting the grass on campus so that it's fresh for when orientation starts. I love the smell of fresh cut grass. I love the hum of a lawn mower in the distance. It always makes me think of when I was kid and our own lawn mower could be heard regularly during the summer. I see the university also has its sprinklers on this morning.

It's a beautiful campus. It really is. I went to school here not too long ago actually. Four years maybe?

It's strange to think about. It seems like just yesterday I was stressing about final exams and what I was going to do with my life after I graduated. I don't miss those days one bit, though I do miss some of the friends I'd made that have since moved away to start their lives elsewhere. I like it here too much, so I chose to stay.

I get to work just in time. Sarah is getting out of her car so I stand on the sidewalk and wait for her. We walk in together.

The day starts off noticeably slower than yesterday, but I don't mind, not this early into my being here. The only downside is that the day feels like it's going by a little slower, and so it feels like it's taking longer for lunch to come around. By the time the clock hits 11:30 AM my stomach is as loud as a thunderstorm rolling in.

Noah is standing outside waiting for me. He smiles when he sees me, and then we walk upstairs together, somewhat awkwardly, I will admit. Are we allowed to be couple-y at work? My guess is that he isn't sure either, since he seems to be acting more shy than usual.

"How'd your morning go?" he asks once we sit down.

I let out a long sigh and lean back.

"I had a lady come up to me with a problem and I totally didn't know how to help her. It turned out okay, though. Sarah saved me."

"She may be a pain in the ass, but she is good at that kind of thing."

"Hey now. She is… actually she is kind of a pain in the ass sometimes, but that's part of her charm."

He laughs.

We eat in silence for a bit. I did *not* bring noodles this time. I know he's already kind of seen me eat in a very unattractive way, but still. It feels wrong to do that now. Unladylike, as my mother would always tell me. Maybe he forgot about noodle day anyway. Hopefully.

"So…" I say, not sure where I planned on going with that.

"So…" he says in return.

"I guess… I-I don't really know… I haven't dated since high school. I don't know what it's like to do this as an adult. Dating in high school was kinda…." My sentence trails off,

"Cringe worthy?" he suggests.

"Yeah. Yeah, I guess that would be the way to put it. Awkward. Way too much PDA."

He laughs. I like making him laugh. Not only is it a sound I like to hear, but I feel like I've accomplished something for some reason. Do I need validation that I'm not screwing this up that badly? I don't know. If it isn't already blatantly obvious, I don't know a lot of things.

"Well," he says, bringing me back to the current moment. "I promise you I won't come to your office to make out with you then. Thanks for ruining my plans."

It's my turn to laugh. He's good at making me laugh.

"Uh, yeah. Please refrain."

"I'll try to contain myself."

I nudge him, gently. He just smiles. That's another thing I like, making him smile. But that's because it's just so damn cute. He is so damn cute. My face is going red. I don't need to be thinking about making out with him right now. *Why did he have to go there*?

"Thanks," I say. "This will be a mutual decision. A mutual containing of ourselves… Well… that probably sounded dumb the way I said that. Sorry."

He takes my hand in his and I'm forced to look right at him. So close.

"It made sense. Nothing to apologize for," he assures me.

"Right. Sorry."

I look down, but he doesn't let go of my hand and so I look back at him. There's a seriousness to the look on his face that wasn't there before.

"Don't be. I like you the way you are. You don't have to try to be perfect. No one is. Also… you *can* say things that don't make sense and I'm not going to judge you. It's just gonna be cute."

"I'm just used to peo…. Never mind. It's not important. Not right now."

There's a sad look in his eyes now, like he already knows what I was going to say.

"What is important right now," he says, "is that our lunch time is sadly up and we actually have to go back to our jobs now."

I look at the time on my phone. Dammit. He's right.

"I look forward to these breaks being an hour when the school year starts."

He leans in to give me a quick kiss, but doesn't pull away right away.

"Me too," he whispers instead, and then he kisses me again.

His lips moving against mine. I can't. I'm pretty sure when he finally does back away he can tell what he's doing to me, because that smile is borderline a smirk this time. Sir, you cannot do this to me. I still have four hours left to my work day.

Everything Is Alright

Chapter Twelve

There's still a big smile on my face when I get back to the office.

"Don't even ask!"

Sarah's practically on the edge of her seat.

"Oh, come on. It's your first lunch together as a couple."

Hearing the word couple sounds weird to me.

"I'm not going to be giving you a play-by-play of my relationship," I tell her.

She gives me a disappointed look.

The word couple rings in my ears for the rest of the day. Is it official? Can we call ourselves that already? I thought there was a period of time before you were considered a legitimately dating *couple*. Maybe that was just a thing in high school and college….

I don't know, but feels like it puts pressure on the whole thing. I know he said I don't need to try and act like I'm perfect around him, but… what if he gets to know the real me and changes his mind? I do often tend to be a disappointment to people. Can I act like everything's okay both at work and when I'm with him?

I'm going to screw this up.

I know it.

I try to shove those thoughts aside and focus on my job. The phone rings, startling me.

"SMU Admissions, this is Charlie."

"Oh… um… hi. I was just calling to check on the status of my application. I know that, like, you can do that online, but I can't seem to log in and… and it's really important to me so I'm just too excited to wait to get a letter or something. Sorry about that, if I'm being annoying."

"No worries. You're definitely not being annoying. I can look that up for you. What's your name?"

(Insert kid's name)

"Date of birth?"

(Insert Birthdate)

"Let me see here…" I look him up in our system and am happy to see that he's been admitted. Sometimes I get calls from people who have been denied and I *do not* want to have to give someone that news. "Looks like you were admitted as of yesterday. You should be getting a letter in the mail very soon."

"Oh my, God, really?"

"Yep."

I can hear him telling his family. Judging by the number of voices I hear congratulating him, they're *all* there with him.

"Sweet! Thank you so much! And have a good rest of your day."

"Thanks. You too."

He doesn't say good-bye before hanging up.

That is something I really do like about this job. It's easy to tell when someone doesn't think they have what it takes to go to college, or thinks they likely won't even get accepted. I love being able to give those people the good news and hear how happy it makes them. Hear their excitement. I was one of those students myself.

I struggled my ass off in high school and almost didn't graduate on time. Last thing I thought I could do was go to college. At first, I started at a community college, assuming I'd only ever get my Associate's degree at most. Then, somewhere along the way, I ended up transferring to SMU and here I am now.

"So. Can I at least know how it went?"

I knew Sarah wouldn't leave this alone for long. However, after my happy phone call, I'm in more of a mood to talk about it.

"It went well. It was only mildly awkward in the beginning," I admit.

She laughs.

"I can see how it would be, now that you're at work."

"Yeah. It feels a little weird to be too… couple-y here."

There's that word again.

"Has he asked you on an official date yet?"

"No. But it's literally been less than 24 hours. Let's not get ahead of ourselves."

He didn't bring it up at lunch, but I'm sure that doesn't mean anything. It's way too soon to be concerned about that. I'm only thinking about it now, because Sarah brought it up. There's nothing wrong with him not bringing it up yet. There isn't.

That happy mood from the happy phone call is dwindling. I'm always questioning if people actually like me, or if they're just being nice. He wouldn't say something about asking me on our first official date to be nice, though, right? In the long run that would actually be pretty cruel. Noah's not like that… I assume.

I don't know him. I don't know anything about him. He is essentially still a stranger to me. I shouldn't assume anything. But… assuming *good* things about people isn't a bad thing to do, right? I'm not immediately thinking he's guilty until proven innocent. I'm going to hold onto this assumption.

-

The rest of the day goes slower than I expected it to. For some reason, it really feels like the hours are dragging. Sarah and I don't talk about Noah anymore. I don't want to. She's making me paranoid. I don't need to be paranoid.

When I finally get home to Dusty he is lying on the back of the couch in the sunlight. He wakes up when I come in, but then goes back to sleep once realizing it's just me.

"I feel ya, Dusty."

I drop my bag by the door and look around the room.

Have I made a mistake?

My thoughts are starting to run wild. They're spiraling. This is what I feared would happen if I tried dating too soon. I can't handle all these new things at the same time. It's stressing me out, but I love my job and I'm not going to break things off with Noah before we've even had our first date. I just… I need to find a way to relax my mind. Or distract it.

I pick up the toy the feather fell off of. It has a little bell that jingles when I do. Dusty knows exactly what this sound means and he is suddenly more alert.

I shake it.

"Wanna play, Dusty?"

He hops down onto the couch cushions and he gets that look in his eyes, does the self-adjusting that makes it look like he's wiggling his butt, which is both funny and cute. I shake it again and he launches off the couch.

I spend the next twenty minutes or so making him chase the feathery end around the living room, making him jump up to try and get it, letting him "catch" it a few times so he can feel like this isn't all a losing battle. He's a very energetic cat, which is good, because this is the distraction I need. I'm all smiles, laughing, having fun. Dusty is doing his emotional support job well.

It's also good for him. Being in a small apartment, I want to make sure he gets the exercise he needs. Maybe I can train him to be an adventure cat, like the ones people always post about online. I could get him a little harness and take him on walks outside. Maybe he would like that. Or maybe he would hate me for putting a harness on him. Who's to say?

We could go to the beach, though not for the water, just the view. And he could climb on rocks and lie down in the sand. I'd have to get all that sand out of his fur after, but it would be worth it.

When he's finally tuckered out I pull out my phone and immediately start looking for a cat harness and leash. I don't even think about it before hitting "Place Order." Don't know if you don't try.

"You'll get to go outside, Dusty. I really hope you like it."

He listens and I like that. I know he can't understand me, but I talk to him anyway, because otherwise I only have myself to talk to. Those little ear twitches of his reassure me that he's at least acknowledging that I am speaking, and somehow that helps

Chapter Thirteen

The next day at work, I screw up.

It's my first real screw up, and even though it's not that big of a deal, I am a mess.

It's not like I didn't see this coming. Eventually everyone makes a mistake, whether they've been at a job for a week or five years. It's inevitable, because we're human and all, unfortunately. I just wish knowing that made me feel better, but it doesn't.

All I did was forget to notify one of our counselors that their visitor was here for their appointment with said counselor. They actually showed up really early. Their appointment wasn't until 2:00 PM and they got here at 1:18 PM. Normally, we would tell the counselor they were here early and they would simply start the appointment earlier. It's to avoid making the visitors sit and wait if they don't have to.

Sarah caught it and got them in at 1:52 PM. On time, yes, but they hadn't needed to sit around for so long, and that was on me. So of course, I'm sitting at my desk trying not to tear up. I'm an adult after all, or so my birth certificate says. I've been one for a while even. I'm not sure why I have not yet mastered the art of controlling my emotions.

If Sarah notices, she's doing a damn good job of pretending she hasn't. I keep expecting her to ask me what's wrong. I hate when people ask me what's wrong. That is a guaranteed way to make sure I *will* cry.

I can't hide it from Noah, though. He notices I'm quieter than usual when we go to lunch together.

"Everything alright?" he asks.

I nod, because I have a hard time being honest about these things.

"Yeah. I'm fine." Even though I don't look at him, I don't need to in order to know he's looking at me. I can feel it. He's studying me. He knows I'm lying, so I don't wait for him to say anything more. "Maybe I'm not."

"What's wrong?"

I was mentally prepared for this question, and yet it still hits me. My eyes start to water.

"I messed up at work," I tell him.

I explain the whole situation, fully expecting him to laugh or tell me I'm overreacting or something. But he doesn't. He's quiet for a moment, thinking it through.

"I'm sure it's an overwhelming job at the start, considering how busy your office typically is. There's a lot of information to take in and learn, a lot of people and situations you'll only get comfortable with after they've happened. You work with good people. Understanding people. Always try to remember that."

I'm mostly just sniffling. I've managed to dry my eyes, though I'm sure they're still red.

"Thanks. I'm just… I'm afraid."

"Of what?"

Can I tell him? It feels too early to dump that I'm mentally unstable on him. Then again… if we stay together he's going to find out anyway.

"My junior year in high school I got kicked out of a class for being too disruptive. I was mad because I got blamed and punished for talking when it was my friend who wouldn't shut up. I was just trying to stop her. I got really pissed. Threw my shit at the new desk I was assigned to. Dropped my heavy book on the desk. Started tapping my foot and my pencil at the same time, angrily. Wouldn't continue reading. That probably sounds like nothing much, but my teacher didn't agree.

"Got kicked out of class in college because I was in a bad mood, even though I hadn't done anything wrong. I just didn't look happy. I was having a rough day. I also cry too easily, like when I mess up at work, even if the mistake is small. I'll cry if someone even remotely sounds like they aren't happy with me. Or looks like they aren't.

"I get really mad easily, even if I'm otherwise super happy. The smallest of things can piss me off.

There are times where I just can't sit still and be quiet, because I'm too happy and too energized.

"I'm telling you this because it's not like you wouldn't eventually learn it anyway. I mean, why hide stuff while you're dating, right? Why not just drop it all at the start so you both know what you're getting into? Well… I'm very emotionally unstable."

I'm not sure how he's going to react to this. It surprises me when he smiles, though.

"I'm bad at caring for myself." he tells me. "I spend so much time trying to make other people happy, regardless of what it costs me. I'm usually pretty exhausted by the time I get home. More often than I'd like, I can't bring myself to make dinner, so I'll either not eat or make something that only requires a micro-wave.

"There are other things too. I have my own issues. I'll save them for a later date, though. I don't think we have enough time left to get into them right now."

"I do that too," I admit. "The dinner thing. I'm too tired to make anything else a lot of the time."

He smiles.

"Everyone has their own problems, Charlie. Some of us are just better at hiding it. Don't think you have to hide parts of yourself to avoid scaring me away. You're right after all. Why do we even try to hide the parts of us that we don't like? They're going to come out.

It's inevitable. If we're waiting to make sure someone feels too strongly about us to back out at that point, well… seems wrong, doesn't it?"

I nod.

"Yeah. You're right. And if you don't like me for all that I am well… your loss."

I smile, which makes him laugh.

"Oh, don't worry. I like you just the way you are. Flaws and all. I promise."

I could die. I could die *right now* and I would be happy. This beautiful man has just promised me he still likes me even with my flaws, and I can tell he's being honest by the way he's looking at me right now.

"Do you think… Do you think my coworkers will accept me the way I am?" I ask.

He puts his arm around me and pulls me close and I just want to stay here forever. It feels… safe here.

"If they don't, I'll go kick all their asses." He pauses. "Well, to be honest I'll glare at them angrily, at most."

"You've known them a lot longer than you've known me and you'd be willing to be a jerk to them?"

He shrugs.

"I mean, if they don't accept you then they're all nuts. And I'm not sure I want to be around a bunch of nutty people. Think about all the years they've been deceiving me into thinking they're normal. I would be heartbroken. I'd feel betrayed."

I elbow him right in the side, but I'm still smiling.

"I'm asking this as a serious question, you know."

"I do know. And they will."

I mostly pick at my lunch. I can't eat when I'm upset. I just don't have the energy for it.

"Thanks for liking me anyway."

I'm still leaning into him, so he kisses the top of my head.

"You don't have to thank me. I'm not telling you I like you because I believe it's what you want to hear. I'm telling you because it's true."

"Thank… shit. Sorry."

He just laughs.

Chapter Fourteen

I've had my job for like… two-ish weeks and somehow, I also now have a boyfriend. What the hell? How did this happen? Who am I?

I ponder this on my way home, and ponder still after I get there. I ponder it all night, essentially.

Saying the word ponder so many times in a row somehow makes saying it sound weird doesn't it? Some words are just like that, though. Like, people, for example. For me, that's one that gets weird.

People people people people people people people.

It even starts to look weird when put down on paper so many times in a row.

But that's not what I'm really here to talk about.

I feel a little better after talking to Noah. It's easy to feel more relaxed around him. It's just the energy he gives off. He, himself, is actually pretty calm most of the time. You know, when he's not giving people shit. Even if this wasn't my plan, I'm so far glad that things have worked out the way they have.

Everything Is Alright

Dusty is in my lap now. It's the middle of night. I'm a little bit worn out mentally, but not enough to help me sleep. Because of this, I'm still up at 1:00 AM watching TV. I know I should probably at least try to sleep, but I don't want to. I know I'll end up tossing and turning for a while anyway.

Tomorrow/today is Friday. I really wish that I was having this issue on the weekend, not when I have to go to work tomorrow/today. I'm going to be tired as shit. I'm going to need a lot of caffeine.

"I don't know what my problem is, Dusty. Noah may have reassured me, but I still feel… uneasy. You're lucky. I'm pretty sure cats don't have mental illnesses, or any animal for that matter. Pretty sure it's just people. We're so smart, but sometimes I think that's exactly the problem, because we also then have the mental capacity to drive ourselves crazy."

Dusty's purring is helping a little bit.

"In fact, you get to sleep pretty much all day. You have someone to house you, feed you, and clean out your litter box. Where can I get that kind of deal? Well… maybe not the litter box part. Toilets work just fine for me."

Every now and then I feel like I've nodded off, but I look at the clock and roughly five to ten minutes have gone by. It's now 3:48 AM. I'm starting to stress about not being able to sleep and that's causing me to have too much anxiety to sleep.

"I may need to try some form of sleep aid, Dusty."

He's no longer in my lap, but he's still nearby, sleeping at the other end of the couch.

"Tomorrow's… today… is going to be rough."

I'm still awake at 6:00 AM.

My alarm will be going off in thirty minutes.

Everything Is Alright

Chapter Fifteen

I decide to start getting ready early. No use waiting for my alarm to go off since I'm already awake. Pulled an all-nighter in the end. I make sure to feed Dusty his breakfast before I head off to work. I'm not looking as cute as I would like today. I decided to go for comfort instead. Not that I think anyone will care.

When I get to work, everyone's in a more chipper mood than I would like. They're too loud.

"Hey!" There's a pause before Sarah continues where she looks me over. "Good morning."

"Morning."

"Everything okay?"

"Yeah. I'm just tired. Didn't sleep *at all* last night."

"Aw… I'm sorry to hear that. Were you by any chance still thinking about yesterday's mistake?"

I nod.

"Noah did a good job of comforting me, but once I was home alone it just…."

"It's okay. I get it."

She doesn't get it. She doesn't get it at all, but I'm not about to tell her that. Instead I give her the good news. Good news which I have forgotten to bring up until now. Whoops.

"Noah and I are gonna go on our first official date this weekend."

"Are you serious?"

"Yep. He texted me this morning before work." (Early enough that I was still a little delusional with lack of sleep. Hence forgetting.) I totally would have gushed over this otherwise.

"Did he give you details? Where you're going? What you're doing?"

"He said he wanted to surprise me."

"Ugh. Okay. I can wait. But the moment you get back home you need to text me the details."

I mean, I probably will. I don't really have anyone else who will care as much, and I'll want to tell and I'll want to tell someone.

Once again, it feels like the day is dragging on. Partly because I'm tired, even with extra caffeine, and partly because I have a date tomorrow that I'm super excited about. In my head, I'm coming up with all these scenarios, my imagination running wild trying to figure out what Noah could have planned.

Dinner and a movie is too cliché. It's also too predictable. There's no way that could be his plan. I'm also assuming we're not going all out adventurous and going skydiving. Something in between predictable and downright crazy.

God, I haven't been on a legitimate date in a while now.

-

Noah gives no hints when we eat lunch together.

"I'm not ruining the surprise!" he tells me.

"But just a little hint. A tiny, miniscule hint."

"Absolutely not."

"You're no fun."

What am I saying? I like being surprised. Amps up the excitement level that much more. I'm glad he's not willing to give me a hint. If he did, I would be obsessing over it the rest of the day and be likely to figure it out and ruin the surprise for myself.

"Are you feeling better today?" he asks, cleverly changing the subject.

Am I? I think so.

"Yeah."

I don't tell Noah I'm exhausted because I didn't sleep at all last night. I don't want him to worry. Besides… I'm not… *not* fine?

His gaze lingers on me in a way that I know means he's trying to determine whether or not that's actually true. He doesn't push me, though.

"Good. I'm glad."

He looks away from me and… does he look a little sad? Does he know I'm not being 100% honest with him? I literally just told him the other day that we should dump all our issues on each other to get that out of the way, and here I am, still hiding. Natural instinct I guess. I feel guilty, though.

"How are *you* feeling?" I ask. "I feel like I never ask that. I'm sorry."

"It's okay. I don't have a whole lot of interesting things to talk about anyway. I'm alright. Sometimes my job can be a little on the rough side. I want to say most of our interactions with students and parents are usually initiated by something going wrong. It's hard to tell a kid whose family needs financial help to send them to college that there's nothing you can do for them to lighten the burden."

I would not last a week in that office.

"I can imagine how that would be rough."

"Your job is practically the opposite," he says with a laugh as he lightly nudges me. "You get all the excitement."

"But sometimes we do deal with people who have been denied," I remind him. "And that's hard to tell someone as well."

"This is true. Just as our office is capable of making someone happy when we *can* help them."

"I guess you're going to get both sides of the coin either way. Is today at least going well?"

He smiles.

"It is. Especially because I get to see you."

"You see me pretty much every day."

"Yes. And that is why they're *all* good days now."

I roll my eyes. I'm about to say something snarky back to that, but when I look at him I lose my train of thought. Will he ever stop having this strong of an effect on me?

Instead of being a snarky little shit about it I lean forward and give him a quick kiss.

"I have to say it. You may or may not play a big part in what makes me look forward to coming to work," I admit.

Except eventually we have to go back to the part of our jobs where we're actually, you know, working. Thankfully, not even frustrated parents can wipe the smile off my face. I have it for the rest of the day.

Everything Is Alright

Chapter Sixteen

I did get to sleep the next night, though not as much as I would have liked to. Maybe got about three hours in. I'm just too excited about my date with Noah. It takes me about an hour and several trial outfits to find something suitable to wear. He texted me and told me he'd come get me at noon. I've been instructed to wear comfortable shoes, so I'm a little curious as to why. My assumption is there will be a lot of walking involved. It's the only thing that would make sense to me.

Right on time, he shows up in a jet-black Nissan Pathfinder. My mother used to have one of those a long time ago. It was her favorite car. He clearly has a much newer model, though.

My heart is hammering in my chest when I get in the passenger side.

"I'm not sure what I pictured you driving, but somehow this isn't it. You don't seem like a black car kind of person," I say.

He laughs.

“I mean, it’s not my favorite color, but I don’t mind it. It’s the color they had in stock.”

“Maybe someday I’ll be able to afford to buy a car right off the dealership lot, but I don’t see that happening any time soon,” I say.

I look out the window as we’re pulling out of the parking spot. Though it is the nicest car I’ve ever owned, my car is still twenty years old. It has its problems. I’ve never had a car that wasn’t at least over a decade old.

“My uncle once told me they’re not guaranteed to be more reliable,” he tells me. “They can have problems right off the lot. Sure, your odds are better, but cars were also made better back in the day… well, in my opinion anyway. It feels like now they care more about how it looks, and the fancy things it can do that aren’t driving.”

“You’re not wrong,” I say in agreement. “My car’s getting close to hitting 200,000 miles and it still runs well. I’ve seen much newer cars not make it nearly as long. Though, that also makes one wonder how people are treating their cars. Sometimes it’s definitely user error.”

“Also true.”

“So where are we going?” I ask.

“Downtown. Grab the bag I left in the back seat.”

Against all traffic laws, I have to take my belt off to reach back that far. I make sure to put it right back on when I’m back in my seat. It’s a black bag. Not super heavy. Because I'm assuming it's what he meant for me to do, I unzip it. There are two compartments separated by a thick divider, a camera in each.

"This doesn't answer my question," I tell him.

He just laughs.

"It's a hint, not a full answer. There has to be some kind of surprise element to it."

"Does there, though?"

He shrugs.

"I think it's more fun, but I will note for the future that you are not particularly patient when it comes to surprises."

We pull into one of the free parking lots downtown. Noah instructs me to take one of the cameras while he takes the other. Then he pulls some kind of list out of his pocket. It starts to click in my head.

"Is this a scavenger hunt?" I ask

He smiles.

"Why yes, it is."

"What kinds of things are we looking for downtown?"

He hands me the list.

Your favorite downtown restaurant.

Somewhere you haven't been yet.

The place you go the most.

Your favorite book.

Favorite local shop/store.

Something that makes you happy.

A place with good memories.

Something that is your favorite color.

A car you really like.

A person you think has the best outfit you've seen today.

"This is actually a really creative idea for getting to know someone. I like it."

"I'm glad to hear that. Let us start then! Number one."

My favorite downtown restaurant is a place that makes *the* best pizza. They have a lot of other things on the menu, but the pizza is what most people know them for. They make it in house with fresh, quality ingredients. Nothing frozen or microwaved. Noah's favorite is the Chinese place, which I will admit comes in a close second for me.

Instead of simply taking pictures of the restaurants, we each stand outside our choice and do stupid poses or make funny faces. I'm hesitant at first, because acting weird in public is something I typically try to avoid, but he volunteers to go first, and seeing how unafraid of what other people might be thinking he is gives me the courage I need.

It turns out to be super fun. We get so many laughs from these photos. Plus, we can talk casually on our way to each destination, so it's pretty low key. Nothing too crazy. Nothing too fancy. My kind of style, really.

We get to "a place with good memories."

“So, what is it that made you choose this place?” I ask.

We’re standing outside the library. It’s a large, pale gray, brick building with concrete steps. Admittedly, I’ve only been to it a few times, even though I do love to read.

When he doesn’t answer right away, I look over and realize he must be reliving those memories right now. He notices me look over at him, though.

“Sorry,” he says. “My mother used to bring me here a lot when I was in elementary school. My dad’s thing was bringing me to the university's hockey games. This was my mother’s. We’d pick a new book each time and she would read it to me.”

“You sound like you’re really close with your parents.”

He nods.

“My whole family, really. I have an older sister and a younger brother. Our parents had activities for each of us. It was their way of making sure they got time with each kid individually outside of the things we did as a whole family.”

“That is so sweet.”

I’m pretty sure his cheeks are turning just the slightest shade of red.

“Yeah. I guess so. It was always just how we did things. When I was *really* little I didn’t even realize that it wasn’t how every family worked.”

"My family didn't work like that," I say. "but we're still close. We've always been there for each other. I shouldn't say that like we aren't anymore. We still very much are. I have an older brother and sister and a younger brother… And you know what? We need to go inside for this one."

"We do?"

"Uh, yeah. We're gonna take the picture right where your mother would take you."

"What if there are other families or kids there? I don't want to seem like a creep taking pictures with strange kids."

I laugh.

"Don't worry. If that's the case, we're just going to ask people to let us interrupt for a moment to take a photo. They can move."

He still seems reluctant, but he follows me inside regardless. The library is filled with shelves upon shelves of books. There's a whole second floor even. The kid's section is on the first floor, all the way in the back corner. There is one mother reading a book to what looks like her own two children, who stick close to her, and a few other random kids whose parents seemed to have dropped them off there.

"Excuse me," I say quietly. The mother looks at me. "Um… would it be okay if we interrupted for a few seconds, just long enough to take a picture. It's for a scavenger hunt."

She looks at both of us. *Really* looks at Noah.

"Oh, okay. Sure."

She gets up and ushers all of the kids, even the ones that aren't hers, off to the side. Noah goes and awkwardly sits in the chair the mother had previously occupied. He smiles for the photo, but his face is totally red, and he gets up the second I say we're good to go. He apologizes to the mother and the kids. The mother just smiles and tells him it's okay. And with the way she's looking at him, I don't think she minds one bit that he interrupted them.

Everything Is Alright

Chapter Seventeen

"A person you think has the best outfit" is kind of an odd one. At first, I want to just take it without them knowing, but then I think that sounds creepy, so I go up to the girl I find and ask if she'd mind helping us out with our scavenger hunt. She's flattered when I tell her it's because I think she has the best outfit I've seen today.

Mine's a very modern look, something stylish that's considered "in" right now. Noah goes for a different kind of favorite. This person's outfit is his favorite because of how unlike everyone else's it is.

The girl he finds is dressed up like a porcelain doll in a lacey dress. Make-up and everything. Her hair is in ringlet curls. She did a great job. And of course, she's super willing to have her picture taken. Noah and I get our pictures taken with our chosen people.

Apparently, she's really into cosplay, but decided dressing "normal" was boring, so now she wears extravagant outfits and costumes all the time. Makes me wonder what she does for a living where they allow her to dress like that. Must be a pretty cool place.

I could never dress in a way that would make me stand out so much. I used to when I was younger. I used to love it at the time. It's kinda hard to believe. Now, I would hate all of the attention. I watch people stare at her as she walks by, do double takes and point her out to their friends.

When we're done with our scavenger hunt, which includes a small intermission for a snack, Noah brings me back home.

"That was really fun," I tell him. "A good idea for a date, too."

"I'm glad you had fun. I did too." He's quiet for a moment. We're still sitting in his car out in my building's parking lot. "It's been a while since I've been on one."

"Me too." I lean forward and give him a quick kiss. "I'll see you on Monday, then."

"See you Monday."

I practically jump out of the car, wave, and then run upstairs. Hopefully that doesn't make it look like I'm trying to flee quickly. I'm just really excited to fangirl over this date. Dusty's going to hear all about it, even though he won't understand a word I'm saying.

Once I'm back in my apartment I hurry to my bedroom and faceplant into my bed, squealing like a little kid in a candy store and flailing my arms and legs around. I sit up and take a breath afterward. I'm so happy right now I can barely contain it. Even though it's later in the day, I'm wide awake and have seemingly all the energy in the world. I could do laps around my apartment complex. Many of them. I'm so happy I can barely sit still.

No, I *can't* sit still.

I need to keep moving.

What can I do, though?

Dusty's watching me as I flit around the apartment. I didn't realize it was getting a little messy. That's what I should do. I should clean. And while I clean, I'll tell Dusty all about my date. I start with my bedroom, which is, unarguably, the worst offender. Then the bathroom, which is attached to my bedroom. Then the living room. Then the kitchen.

Oh! I should also do my laundry. That's been piling up after all.

I pick stuff up off the floor, make my bed, start my laundry, vacuum, do the same in the living room, move laundry over to dryer, move to the kitchen, clean out refrigerator, wash dishes, sweep the floor, dry dishes and put them away, go down to collect laundry, and then fold and put away said laundry, all the while talking to my cat. By the time I'm done, I'm out of breath.

Shit.

It's also past 12:00 AM and I haven't eaten yet. Guess I'm eating late. I can't make something, though. I just washed all my dishes and cleaned the kitchen. I'll order something. $20 for a single meal is absurd, but worth it when you *really* don't want to make food yourself. Plus, I usually only eat half at a time. That's two separate meals, making them $10 each, which isn't quite as bad. I feel that justifies my decision.

I sit down and turn on the TV, watching some detective show as I wait for my food. I've ordered from a local Thai restaurant.

Dusty is purring in my lap, eyes closed as I pet him. He's a little spooked when he hears knocking on the front door. I pick him up and put him on the couch seat next to mine so I can go get my dinner.

Once I get back to the couch, he's all over me. I ordered teriyaki chicken and have to keep pushing him away as he tries to grab at the container.

"Dusty, this is not for you. This is not kitty food."

I'm almost done eating by the time he finally gives up and lies down next to me. When I *am* actually done, I realize it's 1:00 AM. Well, good thing it's only Sunday. It's not like I have to go to work today.

I lie down in bed and try to sleep, but I can't. I'm wide awake. I'm restless. I toss and turn until I decide it's not worth trying any more. It is now 5:00 AM. I may as well have just drunk three whole cups of coffee for how tired I'm… not.

Ok. It's fine. I can just go back to watching TV.

I settle on a baking competition show. I love baking, but I wouldn't say I'm particularly skilled at it. I could never make the kinds of things they make on this show. I wonder if it would be easy to learn. The decorating part would definitely be fun. I like to think I'm artsy.

Dusty moves from my bed to the living room couch, seemingly confused as to why we're still up. He just stares at me for a moment before joining me and lying at my side.

"I think I'm going to teach myself to bake," I tell him. "Can't be *that* hard, can it?"

I look up and save a bunch of recipes for various things and then go online shopping for decorating tools and fancier mixing bowls, because for some reason the ones I own aren't good enough. Might as well throw new measuring cups in. Mine are old. Oh! And a scale. Apparently weighing ingredients is the thing you should do while baking.

"I'm gonna have to go on a grocery run either later today or tomorrow after work," I say out loud. "I'd like to try cake decorating first since I already know how to bake a simple cake. That part I won't have to worry about. I can focus all my energy on making it look good."

I watch TV for three more hours and then start making toast for breakfast. It's going to be a long day.

Everything Is Alright

Chapter Eighteen

I don't sleep a whole lot Sunday night either. Instead, I rearrange the furniture in my living room, reorganize everything in my kitchen cupboards and in the fridge, and arrange the clothing in my closet by sleeve length or lack of. I print out labels for all of the storage boxes in various places in my apartment. I organize my shoes on a new rack I went out and bought earlier in the day.

As hard as I try to go to sleep that night, I'm awake until 3:00 AM. When my alarm goes off at 7:00, I'm not necessarily tired, but I'm frustrated, because I know I should be getting more sleep. On my way out the door, I give Dusty a kiss on the head and say good-bye. He's on the top perch of the new kitty condo I just bought to replace the much smaller cat tree.

-

"Good morning! How'd it go?" Sarah asks as soon as I walk in the door.

I smile as I plop down in my chair, the euphoria from the date still going strong.

"It was amazing," I tell her.

I go over the details for her since I forgot to text her over the weekend. My bad. Luckily, it's a little slower this morning, so there aren't many interruptions. I am surprised by this, though. There's only one more week until classes start. I figured our phones would be ringing off the hook with the last-minute crowd. Maybe it's just too early in the day.

There *are* 78 emails, so I guess that's something. I'm in charge of answering them for the week. I'm happy it gives me a way to stay busy, as I'm still feeling a little restless. Today, sitting at my desk is more difficult than usual. I chalk it up to just being happy. I'm so happy right now. I didn't think having a boyfriend was even something I should put my focus into, but I'm so glad I gave it a chance anyway. I am so fucking happy.

I even put a little more effort into my appearance this morning just for fun, something I almost never do. Sarah notices. Noah does, too, when he shows up. It's only a little awkward now when he comes into our office for legitimate work-related things, because now everybody looks at him differently. It might be in a good way, but you can tell he's still a little embarrassed. Sarah even winks at him, which results in an awkward laugh.

"This is going to stop at some point, right?" he asks.

Sarah just laughs.

"They'll get bored," I assure him. "I'll see you on my lunch break."

"See you then."

After he walks out I turn to Sarah.

"You know you don't have to make him feel uncomfortable every time he comes in here, right?" I ask.

"Oh, I know. But the first few times I'd like to have a little fun with it."

I roll my eyes.

And then everything starts to feel… surreal, in a sense. I keep asking myself how I got here. The happier I am, the less real everything feels. It's like I'm so used to being *un*happy that my brain doesn't know how to process feeling good anymore. And because of this, I keep having to remind myself that yes, I really do work here. Yes, I really do have a boyfriend. Yes, I really do live on my own now. Yes, I really did adopt a cat.

It's hard to explain to other people, though, so I don't bother bringing it up to Sarah when she catches me starting to zone out.

"I was just too excited about everything going on to get good enough sleep," I tell her.

"I can imagine. I'm happy for you."

I'm happy for myself too.

But what if this *is* all just in my head?

What if people aren't experiencing things the way I am?

What if none of this is real and I'm going to wake up in a straitjacket somewhere only to find I was just tripping real bad?

How do I know my mind isn't tricking me?

How do I know any of this actually exists?

I take a deep breath and focus on doing my job.

Lunch with Noah should help. He always helps, somehow.

-

The surreal feeling is still there when I head upstairs.

"You okay?"

Noah's looking at me with genuine concern written all over his face. Do I really seem that out of it?

"I think I'm just tired. I don't know. So much is happening and changing and I just… I'm starting to feel like none of it's real, if that makes sense. I feel like I can't trust my own brain. Like this is all a trick. Everyone is secretly in on some big joke that I don't know about. That I'm going to wake up one day and find out the truth… that none of it was real. Like maybe you're not really here. I'm all alone… It's hard to explain."

I can't look at him, because I'm pretty sure I'm sounding insane and it's still so early in our relationship, if you can call it that, and I'm already fucking this up.

But then he holds out his hand, and that makes me finally look up from the spot on the floor I've been staring at this whole time. Without saying anything, I hold my own hand out and let him take it. He puts my hand on his chest, right where his heart would be, and holds it there.

I feel his heart beating.

I feel my hand moving with every breath in and out.

I feel the warmth that he gives off sitting so close to me.

And I'm okay.

I close my eyes for a moment and focus on those things. Really focus. When I open them again, I'm sitting on the bench that's upstairs, the one on the second floor of the building where I work. I'm sitting here with Noah, a man I just met, but already feel so much for that it scares me a little.

But I *am* here.

And so is he.

"You're not alone," he tells me. "I'm right here."

I can't help it. I can feel my eyes starting to water.

"Thank you," I say. "And this time I really mean it. It's not just an automatic response. Thank you for bringing me back. I'm sorry I am such a mess. I can imagine this is not what you were signing up for."

"Hey now. First, I just want to remind you that I want to get to know you, exactly as you are, whatever that comes with. Second, I understand more than you might think. You're not the first person I've met who struggles with their mental health and you won't be the last. In fact, it's a common problem, sadly. You wanna know something, though? It doesn't make you a bad person, and that's what really matters isn't it? In a sense?"

"What do you mean?"

"I mean, why do we date people? We want to find someone we're compatible with. Someone honest, and kind, and whatever else you want. Just because you struggle with this, doesn't mean you aren't all those things. I know what I'm getting myself into, and I'm not afraid to keep going. I want to give this a chance."

I wipe at my eyes, thankful for waterproof mascara.

"You can't be that understanding. No one is ever that understanding. What's the catch here?"

"You want me to tell you a story?" he asks. "We have time now."

"Uh… sure. I guess."

He takes a deep breath and lets it out slowly.

"I'm sure there's at least a small part of you wondering why I've been single for so long, since everyone made a big deal out of it, correct?"

"Well, yeah, honestly. You're also kinda hot, so…"

He laughs.

"Okay. I guess it's my turn to pray that I won't scare *you* away. Remember how I told you I have other issues? Well, let me explain."

Chapter Nineteen

"I'm very good at hiding my own issues. Sometimes I think a little too good. Anyway, for as long as I can remember, I've had mildly crippling OCD. Obsessive compulsive disorder, if you didn't already know. You likely haven't noticed because I don't eat things that this would apply to, but candy, cereal, chips, any small thing like that, I have to eat in twos. I've dropped a skittle before and then purposefully dropped another one to rectify the 'situation.'

"You won't find a digital clock in my house. I have a piece of cardboard taped over the spot on my TV where ad timers go. I don't like when I look at a clock or a timer and it's on an odd number. It can have an odd number in it. Like say, three forty-six would be okay, but not three forty-seven. So, I'll have to wait for it to change back to even before I can look away.

"I don't have an alarm next to my bed for the same reason, because it will keep me up. I just use my phone instead. I have an even number of just about everything on my work desk. Writing utensils, sticky note pads, paperclips, letter openers, scissors. You get the idea. And sometimes it can cause problems for not just me, but the others around me. Admitting this makes me feel like I sound crazy.

"But yeah, people seem to not like it very much when they have to cater to these things. Admittedly, if you don't count out the whole bowl of chips before trying to hand it to me, I won't take it. This is the case with other easily countable foods as well, which is why I usually do it myself, but the time it takes frustrates others. That little piece of cardboard taped to my tv also bothers people.

"One of the things that can get a little more annoying is if I look at a clock and the time ends in an even number, but then changes before I look away, we have to wait the full minute for it to change again. And then I have to stare at it a bit just to make sure it really is an even number, praying that I don't stare long enough for it to change back to odd.

When you're trying to get out the door, it's a little frustrating to have to stand there and wait. In one way or another, I usually end up driving women insane, so I really haven't bothered looking for anything more than a friend. They're always okay with it at first…."

I lean into him. Rest my head on his shoulder.

"I'm sorry to hear about the way other people respond to that," I tell him. "Thank you for sharing that with me. I'm also really glad you're willing to give me a chance. I know they always say they don't care in the beginning, but I promise you, I really, really promise you it won't bother me. Because… I get it. It's something that's hard to control."

He puts an arm around me and pulls me closer.

"Just like depression and anxiety. Meds or no meds. Sometimes you just have a bad day, or week."

I sigh.

"I'm not going to lie, I probably should be on some form of medication, but I'm too afraid. I hear the lengthy list of potential side effects and all I can think is… why do people risk all of this? And you know what really gets me? When the commercial tells people not to take it if they've had a severe allergic reaction to it in the past. Why? Why *would* anyone?"

He laughs at this.

"I've wondered the same thing." We're both quiet for a moment. Our lunch break is almost over. "If you need someone to ground you back in reality, know that you can always come to me. As long as I'm not in a meeting you can always come find me."

"And actually go into your office?" I ask. "That's uncharted territory. You always come to mine."

I can't see his face, but I can tell he's smiling when he speaks next.

"True. True. I may have to get you a map. Circle my office. Draw a very clear dotted line to it. In red. With an x in the circle to mark the spot."

I nudge him in the side.

"You can shut up now. Seriously. No need to take it that far."

"Like I said, I can be a pain in the ass when I *want*. You got a fair warning far in advance."

"You're lucky you're cute, you know that?"

He laughs again. When I look up at him there's a lingering smile on his face. Then he's serious again.

"Know that I'm not saying things aren't going to be difficult at times. That's just life, regardless of what else you have going on. I will help you, though, if you need it. You don't have to hide how you're really feeling or try to deal with it by yourself."

"I know."

I sit up straight. We gather together anything we brought with us. He gives me a quick kiss on my forehead and then it's back to work.

I feel much better now. I'm back to being "so fucking happy" as I put it earlier. I'm able to focus a little better and go on with my day as usual. I'm not sure what even happened.

I've been there before, suddenly feeling everything I see, or hear, or feel, or know is all wrong. Not real. A place where I feel like I'm actually either the only real person in this universe being tortured with a life of hallucinating shit for God knows what reason, or that I've been committed at some point, and this is all a drug induced trip. It doesn't happen often, but it does happen. I’ve never really paid any attention to if there was something specific triggering it. Maybe I should.

I think about everything Noah told me. I guess it makes sense now. He has his own issues, which I likely never would have noticed if he didn’t tell me, and some people just don't want to deal with dating someone who becomes an inconvenience to them. It makes me sad. He really does understand more than I thought he would. Like they say, can’t judge a book by its cover, but I do it anyway. Shame on me.

I’m just glad he decided to be open with me about it.

Everything Is Alright

Chapter Twenty

Things are going smoothly for the most part. I'm a little more irritable this week. I think that might be because I'm still not sleeping the greatest. My nerves are starting to get to me. It is now the end of the week and the first day of classes is Monday. I know it's likely to be slower now that school is actually in session, but I can't help but be nervous regardless. Something about it makes it feel more official, like I'm not in training mode anymore. I am, but it doesn't feel like it as much.

Don't get me wrong, I'm also very excited. There's nothing quite like the energy of the first day of school, no matter how old you are. Even if you're not even the one going to school, like me, that energy is still there.

As I had predicted earlier, now we are getting all of the last-minute applications, transcripts, questions, etc. I don't mind. It keeps me busy. I don't know how people do it, though. I would be too stressed out. I'm the kind of person that likes my life to be planned out in advance. I'm not spontaneous, to say the least.

If Sarah notices I'm a little more irritable than usual, she doesn't say anything about it, which I appreciate. Noah does, though. But in a way, I still appreciate that too.

"I'm probably just tired, and a little stressed. I'm excited because the new school year starts, but also a little nervous. I'm not sure why, though."

Noah holds on to my hand tightly.

"You got this," he says. "Just remember, things will actually slow down and be a bit quieter. The summer, especially right before the semester starts, is usually the worst of it. In fact, if you can make it through that, you can make it through any other day."

"Thanks. It really does help me a little to hear you say that."

"Always glad to help."

-

I guess maybe Sarah and I don't have a whole lot of time to talk. That could be why she hasn't mentioned it. After all, we're getting inundated with emails and phone calls right now. So much so that I'm already starting to have to be on my own a little bit, though it isn't like I couldn't ask literally anyone else in the office for help if I need it.

"So, how are things going with you and Noah over all?" She asks between phone calls.

"Pretty good, I think. We're really honest with each other, which I think makes a big difference. We try not to hide anything. And we're more alike than I would have expected."

"In what ways?"

"Just that… I struggle with my own things, he struggles with his. I tend to imagine that everyone around me has their life together and I don't, but we share some of the same kinds of problems."

Sarah shrugs.

"I have chronic stomach issues that are brought on by stress and anxiety."

"Seriously?"

"Yeah. If you look around, you'll see more and more people in this office who have or have struggled with depression, anxiety, OCD, PTSD, ADHD, stomach issues, autoimmune diseases. We are all far from being perfect."

"I guess I never looked at it like that. You all hide it so well."

"Well, now you can. Always try and remember that you aren't alone, and that you may relate to those around you a lot more than you think."

"I've suffered from depression and anxiety since I was a teenager," I admit. "It sometimes makes me not the most fun person to deal with, especially when I'm particularly low. I'm amazing right now because of all the newness around me, but there will be a point where I crash, I'm sure of it. Happens every time something new and exciting comes into my life."

“And when it does, know that we have your back. I have your back.”

I smile.

“Thank you. That means a lot. Know that you can count on me too.”

I tell her a little more about how Noah and I are doing before the phone rings again and one of us has to answer it. Since she’s the one to take the call, I sit and think about everything her and Noah have told me. All the things I’d never considered.

I should get professional help. I should stop being afraid.

Chapter Twenty-One

I make a phone call to my doctor's office on my next break. I ask if I can schedule an appointment to discuss some options regarding me maybe taking medication. It's something. I'm not ready to try therapy yet. I thought I was before, but right now I just don't see how sitting around talking to someone about all of my problems could help. Maybe someday.

I'm in luck. She can fit me in the next week. One step done toward bettering my mental health so I don't have to worry so much about losing it in front of people.

Chapter Twenty-Two

Saturday

Chapter Twenty-Three

Sunday

Chapter Twenty-Four

Monday morning comes with a whole new level of excitement. I dress up today, because I want to look especially nice for the first day of my first semester working here. I pre-planned this outfit when I got the job, if that tells you how excited I was for this day. And I couldn't even say why. I'm not going back to school. This isn't an outfit to give all of my new classmates a good impression of me. The people I work with have already seen me.

It's a beautiful day, though. I drive only because I don't want to show up sweaty. The sun is shining and it's a wonderful 65 degrees outside. The high for today is supposed to be 72 degrees, right in the range of perfect. There's a light breeze blowing the leaves in the trees.

I got the chance to sleep in an extra half hour, but I didn't because I was too excited.

When I get to campus I'm greeted by Noah, something that hasn't happened before.

"Everything alright?" I ask him.

He smiles his beautiful smile.

"I just wanted to wish you luck on the first day of the semester. I know how excited you were about it."

"You're too sweet." He smiles again, but this time leans in and gives me a kiss. A good kiss. A kiss harder than all the ones that have come before it. My legs feel like jelly when he pulls away. "Be too sweet," I say, "and you're going to make it hard for me to get through this day, Mister."

He laughs.

"Sorry. We just didn't get a chance to hang out this weekend and I missed you a little bit."

My cheeks burn when he says this.

"I missed you too."

We walk into the building together, but then go our separate ways. When I enter the admissions office, nothing is different, but everything *feels* a little different. There are now students and other staff members all walking about outside that giant window wall, more movement than we've seen out there all summer.

"Good morning!" Sarah says as I walk in.

"Good morning."

I don't know what I'm expecting, but today starts out just like any other day. Sarah is on email this week, so I don't immediately have anything to do until the phone rings.

Thankfully, it's a lady with some very easy questions.

Since high school kids are also going back to school, we definitely don't have as many visitors today. This is okay, though. I log into my own school email and start checking that. It's mostly announcements and welcome emails, but I do note the chat feature off to the side and wonder….

How have I never noticed this before? I can talk to Noah. I mean, I don't want to be a distraction obviously, but maybe I'll just say hi.

CECooper26: Just wanted to say hi and that I hope your day goes well. I realize we focused so much on mine because I'm new, but you have a good day too! :)

NMFoster19: Thank you! :)

I smile to myself as I get back to working, but a little bit later I get another chat message from him.

NMFoster19: I shouldn't be bothering you. Hi again. I didn't tell you how pretty you look today. I mean, you do every day, but especially today. So… Now you know!

Oh, my God. I can't with this man.

CECooper26: Thank you! <3

I close the little chat window before I'm tempted to keep talking to him. There are now people coming into the office that I need to help. I have to remember that I'm here to work. My… boyfriend? Can I call him that already? I *am* already saying couple. Well, either way, he can wait.

But like… not too long.

After I'm done checking people in and helping the few people who came to us to ask questions, I message him back.

CECooper26: Idk how I haven't realized before today that I can message you.

NMFoster19: If it makes you feel any better, neither did I.

CECooper26: It actually does, a little bit. Lol.

NMFoster19: :)

CECooper26: I'm not keeping you from being productive, am I?

NMFoster19: Rest assured, you are not. Most people deal with our front desk more than they ever deal with me, so I'm not super busy.

CECooper26: Good. I would have felt bad.

NMFoster19: Don't worry about it. If I'm answering back that means I would be the one who's just not doing my job. Lol. Still wouldn't be on you.

CECooper26: True. You would just be slacking off, then.

NMFoster19: Exactly!

Sarah notices how much I'm smiling while replying.

"Talking to Noah by any chance?"

"Yes."

"You two are too cute. I love it."

I roll my eyes.

CECooper26: Well I can say the same, so…

NMFoster19: :D

I finally decide to stop bugging him and go back to work, but today there's not a whole lot for me to do. It's just what I expected. Now that most people have been admitted and are attending classes, things aren't going to be so hectic. Which is unfortunate, because I'm having a little bit of a rough time sitting still.

"I'm gonna go on my break," I tell Sarah, and then I change into my walking shoes and grab my earbuds.

Everything Is Alright

I like to go on walks during my breaks. It gives me time to drown out the rest of the world with music and, more importantly, move when I have nothing better to be doing.

It's interesting, walking around campus now that there are students all around me, filling up the hallways, and spending their breaks between classes out on the lawn in the sun. I don't miss being a student. I thought I would, but I don't miss stressing about tests, exams, deadlines, homework, and all that.

The only part of college I really miss is the clubs. That's where I met most of my friends. Now that they've moved away and I'm an adult with a full-time job however, I think my only friends are going to be the people I work with. I really don't have time to meet people anywhere else. I guess, in a way, I should be thankful that a really sweet and cute guy happens to work in the office next door to mine, because I wouldn't have time to try to find a boyfriend anywhere else either.

One of the other ladies I work with happens to be on break when I am and I run into her. I don't know Lydia very well, as she's quieter than most, but she seems really nice, and she did help me with my date, even if she did completely spill the beans on me during it.

"Hey,"

"Oh, hi." She stops and pulls her earbuds out of her ears. "How are you liking it so far?"

I smile.

"I love it. This may be the first and only job I can ever say I look forward to coming to. I mean, yeah, it's still a job, but I like what we do."

"Me too. I'm glad you like it."

"Thanks. And you know it's not just because of like… Noah or anything," I say.

She laughs.

"Oh no! I totally understand," she assures me. "He's just a bonus."

"Exactly. What about you? Boyfriend, married, kids?"

"Married. Five years, two kids. Two boys."

"That must be a handful."

She smiles.

"It can be, but I wouldn't trade it for the world. What about you? Do you want children?"

"I… uh… maybe? I don't know."

There is the whole risk of passing on my mental health issues.

"That's okay. You're still young. You don't need to know that now."

"I'm 30."

"You've got time, Charlie. Believe me."

True. My mother had me when she was 32, but I should probably focus on dating first. Let's not get too ahead of myself now.

I wonder if Noah wants kids.

Everything Is Alright

Chapter Twenty-Five

"Hey! We should totally celebrate your new job and everything. Have you officially done that?" Noah asks me after work as we're headed out to the parking lot.

"No. Not really. What did you have in mind?"

"Whatever you'd like. I know it's a pretty big deal and all. I think you should do something fun."

"Ooh, I know. Ice cream?"

"Ice cream it is!"

We agree on a place and meet each other there. When we step inside, it's like being taken back in time a little. The place we decide on is a lot like the place my family used to go to when I was younger.

It's a tiny little space with tables and chairs for eating and a counter featuring just about every ice cream flavor you could want. Everything is decorated in a simple fashion, white walls with red accents, red, tiled floor.

Noah and I sit at a table in the back, even though there are only two other people here at the moment.

"Thanks for bringing me out," I say.

"Oh, I'm also being a little bit selfish," he admits. "I wanted a second date too."

"Aww. Well, I have no complaints. I'm just glad to hear you wanted a second official date with me."

He smiles.

"And a third, and a fourth, and a fifth, and maybe even a sixth. But that might be pushing it."

"Hey! What's that supposed to mean?" I ask.

"I'm kidding, I swear. I hope for many more."

"Cute. Real cute."

We eat in silence for a bit, but it's not an uncomfortable silence this time. We're just two people enjoying ice cream. Mine's strawberry. His chocolate. Complementary, to most, but I've never been a fan of chocolate covered strawberries. Or chocolate covered anything fruit/berry related for that matter. Ick.

"Do you want kids?" I ask, just throwing it out there. Might as well.

He stops with the spoon halfway to his mouth and stares at me a moment.

"Oh, well... I guess, yeah."

"You guess? I mean, not to judge. I don't really know, myself."

He nods.

"Yeah. I mean, I can picture myself being a dad. I guess I always have. I just never put more thought into it than that, if that makes any sense at all."

I smile.

"It makes perfect sense. I think I'd like one or two. I do have a sort of maternal instinct it seems. I guess I'm just worried...."

"About what?"

"My kid turning out like me."

He sets the spoon down and leans back into his chair.

"What do you mean? I think that would be adorable."

"I mean... because I'm not what people would call mentally stable and I have a lot of anxiety. What if my kid did too?"

He shrugs.

"You wouldn't be alone," he assures me. "You'd have me."

"Oh, you're so sure I'm having them with you, now?"

He laughs, but it's mildly awkward.

"I guess I just did, didn't I. I didn't mean to-"

"It's okay," I tell him. "Just figured I'd get a joke in there as well. To make up for our potentially pushing it with a sixth date."

"I deserved that. But you know what? I'm also serious. If it is me, if this works, I'll be there. It's not something you would have to go through on your own. And even if you're right and your child is like you, well, at least their mother will understand and be able to help them from personal experience. They won't have to go through it alone either."

"I guess you're right." I sigh. "I just... I would hate to know my kid feels the way I do inside, you know? I'd feel like it was my fault."

"It wouldn't be your fault."

"But how would it not?" I question. "How is it not selfish to want a kid even if I know that kid might turn out like me?"

"Because you're allowed to still want that, and because you're going into it with that mindset, and because a million other reasons I can't think of right at this moment. I just know that I wouldn't think you were selfish. There's a chance that won't happen. That's life. Even if you didn't struggle the way you do, your kid still could. It's not a one-hundred percent science."

Noah always knows what to say to make me feel better. How does Noah always know what to say to make me feel better?

"Well, I hope that no matter who it's with, they have that same mindset if it isn't you."

"We would have frickin' adorable children, though. Just saying."

I laugh at that, and then we're both laughing, and I'm okay.

I'm okay.

"You should come meet my cat," I tell him, subtly asking him to come to my apartment without making it sound like I'm suggesting we go start on those kids right away. I'm not. I swear.

"Oh?"

I nod.

"Yes. Before we talk about children I must know if my cat approves of you. If he doesn't, well… sorry."

"Ouch. Okay. I'll come meet him then. I'll follow you."

When we're done I walk outside and get into my car, nearly having a heart attack when I get there. I just asked Noah to come to my apartment. Oh, my God. What was I thinking? It's gonna be difficult to restrain myself with him in my personal space. That thought of us cuddled on the couch comes into my head again. That *nice* thought.

I let Noah know to park in guest parking, and when we finally get back to my place, I wait for him as he parks.

"It's upstairs," I tell him as he walks up to me. I'm not sure why I tell him. He would have figured that out when I started you know, walking up the stairs. Whatever. Not to mention he picked me up before. He likely saw me come downstairs. Why am I this awkward?

I unlock my door and walk in. Noah follows. Dusty is on the couch, but he gets off and runs into my bedroom.

"I hope that's not a bad sign," says Noah, nervously.

I laugh.

"It's okay. He hasn't really met new people. I'm sure he'll come out."

"And in the meantime?"

I brace myself, knowing how hard this is going to hit me, and then I turn around.

Yep.

Smacked right into a brick wall.

Because he's looking at me with a suggestive expression on his face and I am suddenly sweating.

"In the meantime," I say, "you can come over to my couch and get to know me a little better."

I cannot believe those words just came out of my mouth.

"I would like that very much," He responds.

When I pictured Noah in my apartment and on my couch, I did not picture him kissing me. I didn't picture him gently pushing me down so he could climb on top of me. And I sure as hell did not picture me wrapping myself around him like I never wanted to let go. And yet, that is exactly what happens.

This close I can't see anything, smell anything, taste anything, or feel anything else. Noah has a hold on every one of my senses and I wouldn't want to be anywhere else with anyone else doing anything else. It's intoxicating.

To be honest, I would like it if things didn't stop here, but as luck would have it, this is when Dusty decides to come back out of my room and loudly announce his presence to us.

"I think he wants to say hi now," I say.

Noah just laughs, and this close I can feel it.

"Hi Dusty," he says quietly.

We separate and sit up on the couch. Dusty hops up and sniffs at Noah before lying down in between us.

"I think that's a good sign," I tell Noah. "He trusts you enough to be this close. But then, maybe he just wanted you off of me."

Noah laughs again.

"He does seem pretty content where he's at… in between us."

Noah pets Dusty and scratches behind his ears as Dusty purrs up a little rumbly storm. He protests only a little when I pick him up and move him to the other end of the couch.

"Tv?" I ask Noah.

"Sure."

"Care what we watch?"

"Depends on if we'll actually be watching it or not."

My whole self burns.

"Random ass show we don't have to put a lot of attention into it is."

We spend a good amount of time kissing again until eventually he lies down beside me and puts his arms around me so we can cuddle and actually watch the show I put on. Being here is like being inside, wrapped up in a blanket with a cup of hot cocoa in the middle of a winter storm. The utmost level of comfort, warmth and peace.

Chapter Twenty-Six

Sarah is dying about as much as I am on the inside when I tell her about Noah coming home with me the night before.

"So… did you guys, you know…?"

"No! I mean… no. We did not. Not that I wouldn't have, but I think we should wait a little while longer. I'm not really the type to hop into bed with someone right off the bat."

"Well, I'm still super happy for you. I'm glad things are going well.

"Thanks."

"Does Dusty approve?"

"He seems to. He laid by us and let Noah pet him, so I think it's all good. He pretty much gets along with everyone, though, according to the lady at the shelter, so I'm not too surprised."

After a brief conversation about it, we get back to work.

I add my doctor's appointment, which is today after work, to my personal calendar. I don't know why, but I don't tell Sarah about it, even though I would like to talk about it, because I'm nervous. I don't know what to expect. I've been putting it off for so many years thinking that I could handle things on my own.

It's not that I've been scared to go to the doctor. I just… wanted to be stronger than that. I know, it's dumb. Getting help doesn't equate to weakness. In fact, I think I'm making the stronger decision by making the appointment.

The only thing is that I don't feel depressed and anxious all the time. Like, lately I've been fine. I start to question if I actually even need help at all. Maybe sometimes I'm just a little more sad than usual. Sure, it's been crippling from time to time, but I always seem to bounce back.

Then again, I have good things happening in my life. New things. New things in particular always make me feel like I suddenly have everything together and I'm happy and I don't need help. Of course, I haven't been sleeping much, so maybe that's not true? I've also been a little irritable, but I think that's just because of the whole lack of sleep thing.

Either way, I suppose it doesn't matter. I'm going to this appointment. It's only taken me sixteen years to make one after all.

I tell Noah about it at lunch and he's happy for me.

"I'm glad you're getting help."

"I'm nervous," I admit.

"That's understandable when you're going into something with no idea what to expect. It'll be okay, though. I promise."

"How are you so sure?"

"Because I did the same thing," he explains. "I may still have OCD, but it's better than it's been in the past. Or at least, the anxiety part of it is."

"You take medication for it?"

"Yes, and I would never go back to winging it on my own. Sometimes, you just need a little extra help, but that's not a bad thing. It doesn't mean there's anything wrong with you, and you're not weak."

"What about side effects?" I ask. "I'm kind of afraid of that part."

"You don't have to stay on a medication if it's making you feel worse, sick, or otherwise off. You can always change. There are a lot of them out there. I know it would be much easier to say you'll find the right one right away, but you likely won't. Just don't get discouraged."

"I promise I won't," I say.

"Thank you."

He gives me a kiss on the forehead.

We talk about this through most of our lunch together, which is now an hour long. I have too many questions for him. I'm just glad he puts up with them all and answers them with honesty and patience.

The rest of my day isn't very exciting. It's mostly paperwork and helping get stuff out in the mail. It's amazing how much mail we send out. There are a lot of people surprised by the fact that we even send what they call "snail mail," but we actually send quite a bit for various different reasons.

I get it. Pretty much everything is digital. Even the intake paperwork for my doctor's appointment is all online, and they sent it to me to fill out in advance. Most of it's general information, but there's this really long mental health assessment included. This thing is going to take me at least fifteen to twenty minutes to fill it out. I start it toward the end of the day when we've slowed down.

Question One: In the past 6 weeks, how often have you experienced the symptoms below? Never. Sometimes. Most days. Every day.

I was very anxious, worried or scared about a lot of things in my life.

I guess I have been kind of anxious lately. Most days.

I felt restless, agitated, frantic, or tense.

Um… a little? I guess sometimes.

I had trouble sleeping - I could not fall or stay asleep, and/or didn't feel well-rested when I woke up.

Lately? Most days.

A lot of the symptoms didn't apply to me at all.

My heart would skip beat, was pounding, or my heart rate increased.

I don't think my reactions to Noah count in this case.

I was sweating profusely.

My hands, legs or entire body were shaking, trembling, or felt tingly.

I had difficulty breathing or swallowing.

I had pain in my chest, almost like I was having a heart attack.

I felt sick to my stomach, like I was going to throw up, or had diarrhea.

I felt dizzy, my head was spinning, or felt like I was going to faint.

I had hot or cold flashes.

I was scared that I would lose control, go crazy, or die.

Some of them applied to me a lot at the time being.

I experienced an unusually elevated mood where I was extremely elated, energetic, or irritable.

I had periods of time when I needed little or no sleep, yet functioned as well as or better than usual.

My mind was flooded with thoughts, and I talked more/faster than usual.

I started to tackle multiple goals/activities at once (more than I usually would) or jumped from one interest to another in an attempt to do it all.

I got involved in fun things that, in hindsight, could have had negative consequences (e.g. carefree or unprotected sex, shopping sprees, unwise investments, excessive gambling, etc.)

Some of them applied to me in the past for sure.

I felt slowed down compared to my usual pace.

I felt exhausted.

I felt worthless or guilty.

The sadness I was feeling made it difficult for me to function in my personal, social, or work life.

I experienced extreme mood swings from depression to elation without any apparent reason.

I frequently felt sad, like I couldn't go on.

I definitely have no substance abuse, so no to all of that. Hmm… I didn't know feeling good and being productive could be considered a symptom of anything. The more you know, I guess.

I fill out all the general information and then hit submit.

"What's that?" Sarah asks.

"Oh. I have a doctor's appointment after work, this is just a pre-check in."

That's all I say. I'm still not willing to tell her what the appointment is for, even if we *have* already talked about the fact that I have personal issues I'm dealing with.

Everything Is Alright

Chapter Twenty-Seven

I pull into the parking lot of my doctor's office gripping my steering wheel harder than is necessary. I always had just a little bit of anxiety about going to my doctor. I mean, who likes doctor's appointments? Pretty sure the answer to that is no one.

The doctor I go to is in a small office with a few others. When I walk in I check in and sit down in the waiting room. A small office is nice. It's less people and everything isn't sterile and white. I mean… it's probably sterile, but I don't mean it in a literal sense. It's much cozier, to put it simply.

I wait for maybe ten minutes before a nurse comes and gets me.

"Charlie?"

She takes my vitals, asks me a few questions and then I'm left to wait for the doctor to come in. I can't help but look around. I always wonder if they secretly have cameras in here somewhere. Like maybe they want to see what people do when they have to wait for any given amount of time. I could totally be a part of a secret social experiment right now.

But that's not likely. I don't know why I'm even thinking about it. Except now that I am, I can't *stop* thinking about it, or looking around the room to see where there may be a small camera hidden.

A knock sounds on the door a moment later and a tall, thin woman with blonde hair walks in the door. She looks like what I imagined Noah would go for.

"Hi Charlie. What brings you in today?"

What brings me in? Pretty sure my intake forms clearly answered that question already.

"I've been struggling with my mental health for a while now. Mostly depression. I guess I'd finally like to try and do something about it."

"Okay, well, let's see where you're at. How do you feel right now?"

"Oh, well, right now I feel great! Actually, I feel pretty amazing. Everything's going well. I have all my motivation and energy. There are no complaints. It's just… I'm not always like this. Sometimes I'm sad all the time and I think lowly of myself. My confidence is low and I just don't want to do anything."

"How you feel right now, does that tend to happen between periods of being depressed? Is it normally one extreme to the other?" she asks.

"I guess you could say that."

As I'm talking, she's typing things into her computer. I wish I knew what she was typing. Why is she focusing so much on how I feel right *now*? That's not what I came in for.

"Are there other things you normally feel or do when you're in this state? Any risky behavior, excessive spending, irritation, hypersexuality, and so forth?"

"Well… I am easily irritable, but I think it's just because I'm not getting a whole lot of sleep. You could say I've been spending more lately, but I don't necessarily see it as excessive."

"I see."

You see what? I wonder.

"I just got a new job and a boyfriend and a cat, so that's probably why I'm feeling like I do right now, but that's not really why I came in here," I finally tell her.

"Right. You came in because of feelings of depression. Do you feel as though your lack of sleep is bringing you down, slowing you down at all?"

"No."

"I see."

There she goes again with that. What do you see, lady? What do you see?

"Well?" I ask. "Can I be put on something to fix this?"

-

After a little more talking she sent in the medication right away so I could go pick it up at the pharmacy after my appointment and get started immediately, though she did suggest taking it in the morning would be better, so I would have to wait until the next day anyway.

I called Noah afterward to tell him about my new medication and to get moral support. The first thing I did when I got home was Google all of the side effects and let me just say I should not have done that. If this one doesn't work I'm going to have to remember not to do that for the next one.

I'd never taken medication for anything, though. I don't know if I'm sensitive to them or not. Most I've ever taken is a pain killer, but the side effects of those are almost nonexistent for the most part. At least, it's typically unheard of that someone ended up in the hospital or at the very least feeling sick and disoriented because they took a Tylenol.

Chapter Twenty-Eight

I take my medication early the next day and then get ready for work. My doctor said it should take roughly four to six weeks to really know if it's working or not, so I don't expect much right away. I'm just hoping that it doesn't come with any of the side effects listed on the side of the bottle, and there are a lot. Like… A LOT.

It would be easy to question why anyone would risk this, but I guess sometimes the benefits can outweigh the side effects. If I do get anything, I hope that's the case.

I want to say I'm optimistic overall. There's a chance that I may actually feel better. This is great. This is what I want. I'm just still so nervous. I try not to think about it when I go into work.

"How'd your doctor's appointment go?" Sarah asks once I've sat down at my desk.

"Good," I say. "I'm healthy."

Kind of a lie, but oh well. I probably am physically healthy, in all actuality.

We have a few more people than we did the day before, but still not too many. I'm glad things have officially slowed down a little. It makes learning the job so much easier. I feel like I can finally breathe again.

I open up my computer and log in using my phone. Since I don't have anything to do right away, I go to our school's web page and look around a bit, familiarizing myself with other departments. Because that's the thing. Our office is practically the same as an operator. Everyone calls us for everything. It's good to have a basic knowledge of the school as a whole, not just our own office.

"Hello," I say as a family walks into the lobby.

"Hi. We're here for a tour?"

They say it like it's a question. We actually get that a lot. Maybe we're not clear enough about where people need to be.

"Yep, you're in the right place. I'll let them know you're here."

"Thank you!"

Easiest part of my job by far. This family seems excited too. Okay, most families do, but some a little more so than others.

-

Time moves by a little more quickly from here on out. It's lunch time before I know it.

"I started my new medication today," I tell Noah. "My doctor was considering a few options, but we finally decided on an antidepressant and an as needed anti-anxiety med."

"Sounds good. What else was she considering? Do you know?"

"She's not entirely sure that I'm just depressed. Apparently, I'm doing too good right now and it's suspicious to her or something? I don't know. She kept questioning it, but I assured her that I'm usually not like this, and that my life is just going really well right now."

"I see."

I give him a look.

"What?" I sort of snap. "She kept saying that too. What do you guys see?"

"I-I didn't mean it like that. I'm just saying-"

"Do you think there's something else wrong with me?" I ask, cutting him off.

"No. No. I was just… as long as you're doing well, that's all that matters right?"

"Right."

He leans over and pulls me into a hug, one I don't reciprocate right away.

"I'm sorry," he says. "I didn't mean to suggest that I thought maybe there was something more to it than that. I'm not a doctor. What do I know?"

I finally hug him back.

"It's okay. I'm sorry I kind of snapped. It's just… I'm not crazy."

"I don't think you are."

"My doctor does, "I tell him.

"What do you mean?" he questions.

"She thinks I might have bipolar disorder."

He looks at me for a moment without saying anything.

"That doesn't mean you're crazy, Charlie."

I can't help but laugh a little.

"I read about it online last night. I'm not like that. I don't have psychotic episodes or anything like that."

He shrugs.

"Not everyone with that disorder does. It's more of a spectrum in reality."

"But it makes me sound crazy."

He sighs.

"I wouldn't look at it like that. Besides, that's not what she's treating you for, right? You could just suffer from depression, but you're doing particularly well right now. Let's just focus on that, okay?"

"Yeah. Okay. I guess you're right. We'll see how this medication goes and go from there. She did say, though, that it could make things worse if it's not just depression."

"Worry about that bridge when or if you get there. For now, I would stay hopeful. I think you're doing a very brave thing."

"Thanks. That means a lot."

I return to work in the same mood I started, optimistic. I do think more about what my doctor talked about with me, though. What if she's right? Noah says that doesn't make me crazy. But doesn't it? I've seen shows and movies and how they depict people with bipolar disorder. I'm not like that… am I?

Now I really don't want to talk about this with Sarah or anyone else. I don't want them to judge me, and surely, they will.

-

It's later in the day. I'm home now. I play with Dusty for a while before settling into my couch to watch some TV. I need a distraction. Except… it doesn't distract me. I pull out my phone and scroll through page after page of information regarding this disorder and I can't lie. A lot of it does sound like me.

I'm not promiscuous, but there are times where I think about sex pretty much constantly, and have a hard time… uh… managing it. So maybe hypersexuality does fit to some degree.

I do get kind of loose with my money from time to time. Especially lately. I keep buying more things for my apartment and for Dusty, things I probably don't need. The harness is a bust so far, by the way. I put it on him and he just flops over onto his side and doesn't move. I'm not sure I'll have an adventure cat.

I still haven't used all of the baking stuff I got either. In fact, I haven't even taken any of it out of the boxes the stuff came in. I keep telling myself I will, but I just get distracted by something else I need/want to do.

I did clean my whole apartment not too long ago. And label everything. So, there was definitely some heightened productivity, plus the extra energy. All this, even though I haven't been getting a whole lot of sleep.

Maybe I'm wrong.

Maybe my doctor's right.

I'm scared.

I keep scrolling. I can't help it. I even go to message boards and start reading about other people's experiences. They sure do sound like me. I end up scrolling through post after post until it's after 10:00 PM. I should try to go to bed, even if I don't think I'm going to get much sleep.

-

My dream tonight is a nightmare.

I'm screaming at my parents, they're screaming back at me.

I'm crying.

I'm throwing things.

Breaking things.

Destroying everything around me.

Hurting everyone I love.

They hate me.

I've made them hate me.

-

I wake back up some time in the middle of the night, covered in sweat. Dusty is lying next to me, and startles awake with me. He looks up at me, his yellow-green eyes asking me questions he can't speak. Why am

I awake so suddenly? What's wrong? Why do I look scared?

I roll over and put my arm over him, giving him a little hug. He goes back to sleep, but I can't. I'm awake until my alarm goes off the next morning.

Everything Is Alright

Chapter Twenty-Nine

The next few days kind of suck. I have this headache that won't go away and I'm feeling a little nauseous. At first, I think I'm coming down with something, but then I remember it could be my new medication. Ugh.

I go into work anyway, though the days seem to last forever and I feel gross. I put no effort into getting ready for work beyond what is necessary. Everyone seems to notice, but nobody says anything to me. Not even Noah. He just holds me at lunch time and lets me close my eyes for a moment. I'm almost falling asleep by the time I have to go back to work.

While I was on my lunch break Anna gave Sarah and I some side work to do when we're not busy and I grumble about it the whole time. I'm still trying to learn my job. Why can't she just let me focus on that? Why does this shit need to be done so urgently? *Does* it even need to be done so urgently?

"Everything okay?" Sarah asks me on the third day.

"Yeah. Everything's fine."

"Are you sure? You seem-"

"I said I'm fine!" I practically yell at her.

She looks at me with a completely shocked expression. I can't blame her. I'm shocked, myself.

"I'm sorry," she says. "I just wanted to be sure you're doing alright."

"Thanks… I'm fine," I repeat for the third time.

I grab my phone and my earbuds and leave the office. I need a small break, that's all.

I don't run into anyone this time, which I'm thankful for. I let the music drown out the rest of the world. I could dance to it without a care in the world, be the star of my own music video. I'm famous. I'm happy. I'm free. I want to stay in this fantasy life my brain is conjuring up forever.

I open my eyes and realize I *was* actually dancing along to the music and people are staring at me. My cheeks burn. I duck my head and keep walking, moving away from everyone so they can't see how clearly embarrassed I am.

What the hell was I just doing?

By the time I go back to our office I'm in a better place. Embarrassed, but also not so crabby. I apologize to Sarah for snapping at her. She forgives me. I also explain that I'm not feeling the best, but I don't tell her why.

"I'm sorry to hear that. Anything I can do to help?"

"No. I'll be fine, but thanks."

How many times have I said the word fine today?

I go back to work, pretending nothing happened at all. I make sure to update Noah when we have lunch, though. I don't think he'll judge me.

We sit upstairs in our usual spot. I'm leaning against him, with my eyes closed. I open them and stare at the carpet on the floor and really look at the pattern for once. It's an ugly carpet.

"Does the medication seem to be doing anything yet? Or is it still way too early to tell?" he asks me.

"I think it's still too early to tell. At least, I don't feel any different. Mostly just sick and grumpy."

"I'm sorry to hear that. I hope you feel better soon."

"Thanks." I take a deep breath and let it out slowly. "You wanna do something fun after work?" I ask.

"Like what?"

"I don't know. Anything. You pick."

He thinks about it for a moment.

"You sure you're feeling up for it?" he asks.

I nod.

"The side effects only seem to last a very short period of time each day," I explain.

"You should eat then," He suggests. "You skipped eating at lunch. What do you feel like?"

"Somehow this seems to be turning around to make me be the chooser."

He laughs.

"Yeah. I kind of am turning it right back to you, but I'm serious. What do you want?"

"Chinese?" I suggest. "We can get take out and watch a movie. I get anxiety eating in restaurants, so I'd prefer to be home."

"Chinese it is then."

He orders ahead at the end of the day so he can pick up the food on his way to my place. I go home and make sure there's nothing embarrassing lying around. I also feed Dusty and hope that he doesn't want to spend too much time trying to eat our food. I don't want to make Noah have to fend him off the whole time.

When Noah arrives, I open the door to the heavenly smells of Chinese food. He picked it up from his favorite place downtown, my second. At this moment, though, I'm not sure why it's not my first as well.

I let him in and he sets the bags down on my coffee table and starts pulling the containers out. Dusty, unsurprisingly, is making his way over to examine the food we have spread before us, even though he literally just ate all of his.

"No, Dusty. You can't eat this food."

Most of it is chicken. I probably shouldn't take my eye off of him for too long. Chicken is his absolute favorite.

I pick a movie from one of the few streaming services I have and hit play. Then, while the credits are playing I get us plates and something to drink. Once we're all settled in we curl up on my couch and wait for the movie to start.

It's a good movie. I picked a comedy, just because I wasn't sure what Noah would like and I figured who doesn't like comedies? Also, I wasn't going to subject him to some chick-flick/rom-com movie. Though for all I know, he could be totally into those.

We eat in silence as we watch the movie. When we're done eating I curl up to him and he wraps an arm around me. I'm comfortable like this, but unfortunately it doesn't last long. Dusty takes his shot and knocks over the sweet and sour chicken box. He grabs a piece of chicken and makes a run for it.

"Dusty! Dammit!"

I figure I'm not going to get the chicken back so I let him have this one. I do, however, make sure to pack up the rest of the uneaten food and put it in the refrigerator. When I get back to the couch, Noah's laughing.

"You gotta admit it was cute, though, the way he tore outta here once he got that chicken piece."

I roll my eyes.

"Yeah, yeah. Whatever. Little shit."

"But he's *your* little shit."

I don't even know where he went and I don't care to. As long as he eats all of it and doesn't leave me a nasty surprise for later.

Before I can sit down again, Noah turns himself and lays down on the couch. He reaches out for my hand and I let him take it, let him pull me down on top of him.

"Is this movie boring you?" I ask.

He shakes his head.

"No. But I think we need an intermission."

"Oh, do we now?"

He's quiet, so I hit pause on the movie. He responds by nudging me so that I lift my head off his chest and look at him. I take the hint and scoot up a little, bringing my mouth to his. I don't think I'll ever get over the way kissing him makes me feel. We could still be together at 80 and I don't think it would change.

I push myself up and look at him. He's staring back at me.

"What?" He asks.

"Nothing. I'm just admiring how cute you are."

He smiles and his cheeks turn pink. He looks away from me.

"Maybe we should go back to watching the movie instead," he suggests.

"Am I making you uncomfortable?" I ask.

He shakes his head.

"No, but I'm trying to be a gentleman here, and if you keep looking at me like that I'm going to want to do a whole lot more than kiss you."

"Oh!" I move back down and rest my head on his chest. "Uh… yeah. We should probably watch the movie in that case."

He sighs and it feels like a sigh of relief. Would it really be so bad? Sure, it's his second time here and we haven't been dating that long, but we're also adults. I respect him trying to be gentlemanly about it by not rushing me. I try not to let myself become paranoid. It's not me. He just wants to take things slowly, and that's okay. I can feel his heart racing underneath my head. I can hear it. It starts to slow back down once we're watching the movie again.

There's still a tiny voice in the back of my head arguing that maybe I'm wrong.

Maybe it *is* me.

Everything Is Alright

Chapter Thirty

I find myself thoroughly enjoying life for once. So far, everything is going so well. With my job. With my apartment. With Dusty. With Noah. Doubts try to sneak their way into my brain, but I've gotten better at shutting them out. I've gotten better at living in the moment and not dwelling on the past, or my unknown future.

Noah helps a lot. I am afraid I'm starting to depend on him a little too much, but he constantly assures me that everything's okay, and I want to believe him. No. I do believe him. He doesn't lie to me. He's not like that.

I'm there for him too, obviously. That counts for something, right? It's not all one-sided, I promise. I understand that he has his struggles too. Sometimes we may say something that rubs the other the wrong way, but we always come to realize what we actually meant. I wouldn't say we ever really fight. We argue from time to time, but not for long.

I know, I know. This may just be the honeymoon phase of our relationship, which will surely end at some point, but I like to believe that there's more to it than that. I like to believe that Noah and I understand each other enough, more than other people understand us, and that will keep us going strong through anything.

But then I start messing up.

-

The day starts out calm and relatively normal. I go to work as always, we have visitors, Sarah is as chipper as always, which boosts my own mood. It's infectious, really.

But I make a mistake.

I mess up and this time it's bigger than the last time. I didn't mail something out that needed to be mailed out today in order to make it to its destination on time and our secretary is pissed at me and I'm pissed at her, because she didn't tell me about it in the first place, so how was I supposed to know?

She practically yells at me in front of everyone else, which, regardless of how I handled things from there on out, was NOT cool. But, uh, yeah… I didn't handle things well at all. I had just picked up the mail and was holding it when she confronted me. I threw it at her feet, said "fuck you, you didn't even say a word about it to me" and stormed out of the room. Real adult of me. I know.

I don't grab my phone or my earbuds, so I can't listen to music. Instead, I just walk angrily, unsure of where I'm planning to go. Unfortunately for him, Noah happens to be walking out of the Financial Aid office. He sees me and follows me outside.

"Hey, is everything alright?" he asked.

"Does it look like everything is alright?" I responded.

"Uh… no. I suppose not. What's wrong?"

"I messed up and our secretary was a bitch about it in front of everyone and I got pissed off at her and swore at her and now everyone in my office just watched me lose my shit. Everything is not alright."

"I see…"

"Do you, though? Do you really?"

"Charlie, please just stop for a second. It's going to be okay."

"You don't know that!"

"Yes, I do. It's not the end of the world."

I don't know why, but him trying to comfort me pisses me off even more. I'm not in the mood to hear it right now.

"You know what? You can screw off too, for all I care. I just want to be alone."

"Charlie, please."

"No. You don't get it. Just leave me alone."

I grab a nearby trashcan and kick it over, right in his path so he has to stop to avoid tripping over it. He stops following me then. I walk to the back of one of the buildings where there are no people and curl up in a ball in the grass, wrapping my arms around my legs.

What I really want to do is tear myself out of this body. I want to rip my skin right open and crawl out, because I'm mad, and I'm *too* mad. I don't know how to handle it. It's just too much. I want to pull my hair out. I want to scream. I want everything to stop. But nothing is going to stop.

I start crying. I start crying, because I want to lose my shit even more, but I also don't want to do it in public. I've had enough humiliation for one day, thank you. So I cry. I cry for a while. I'm not sure how long. Long enough that I should really be getting back to work. I know that much.

I don't want to go back, though. How can I after that?

But I do.

I force myself up off the ground, dry my eyes, and make my way back toward the administration building. I see that Noah has picked up the trash and the can and put it back in its rightful place. God, I feel bad about snapping at him. He's gone too. Probably back to his own office.

When I walk back into mine everyone looks up at me. Some of them look away really quickly, some of them stare for a little bit. Sarah watches me the whole time as I walk and sit back down at my desk.

"I told Erik I'd let you know to go talk to him when you got back," she tells me.

Oh great. When your boss wants to have a word with you that's not usually a good sign. I get up from my desk and walk back to his office on shaking legs. My chest hurts. I knock on his door.

"Come in."

"Hi," I say as I walk in and sit down in the chair across from his desk.

He leans back in his chair and is looking at me with a facial expression I can't read.

"So, I'm sure you know why I've called you in here," he responds.

I nod.

"I'm in trouble, right?"

"No, no. I just wanted to have a talk."

"I'm really sorry. I lost it. And there were people in the lobby."

"You did. What's going on? Are you okay?"

I take a deep breath.

"I don't know. I've been a little more irritable lately, because I haven't been feeling the greatest and I just… she embarrassed me in front of everyone."

He nods.

"It wasn't her place to call you out like that publicly, I will agree. I had a talk with her too."

I look up from where I've been staring at his desk.

"You did?"

"Yep."

"Thanks. Again, I'm so sorry. I promise it won't happen again."

"Charlie, if there's anything you need help with, you can come to me. If there's anything I can do to help…."

"Oh… I don't really think there's anything specific. I just needed to cool down a little bit, which I have."

"I can see that. Look, sometimes people make mistakes. I'm not going to reprimand you for your behavior today, but I do hope that you hold true to that promise."

I nod.

"Of course. Thank you."

"If you feel like you might lose it again, know that you're welcome to come to me. I'm not always the best at giving advice to people, but I've been told I'm a pretty good listener. Plus, I don't care if you cry or you don't talk at all. I just want to make sure you're alright."

"Yeah. Okay. Thanks again, really."

"Well, I won't keep you any longer. Thanks for coming to talk to me."

I don't think I really had a choice in the matter, but I don't say that to him. I just quietly make my way back to my desk. Sarah is still looking at me as I sit down.

"Everything okay?" she asks.

I'm getting sick of people asking me that.

I nod.

"Everything's fine," I answer.

"And you? You're okay?"

"I'm alright, yeah. I just… I don't know what that was. But I'm not gonna let it happen again. I uh… I snapped at Noah too."

She gives me a half-hearted smile.

"I'm sure it's okay. He'll be understanding if you apologize."

"I sure hope so. I threw a trash can in his way and everything."

"Damn."

"I know."

-

I finish out the day without incident. Our secretary and I don't really look at each other, though. Things feel really awkward because of this. I want to apologize to her, but it's not like she has apologized to me, so I'm going to be stubborn and just… not. Again, I know, so adult of me.

At the very end of the day, as I'm walking out of the building, I run into Noah. He's walking to his car. Hearing someone behind him, he turns and sees me.

Everything Is Alright

Chapter Thirty-One

"Hi," is all I can think of to say to Noah.

He stops and waits for me to catch up.

"Hi," he says in return. "Feeling any better?"

"Yeah. I'm sorry about earlier."

"It's okay."

"No. It's really not okay. I shouldn't have reacted the way that I did. I'm sorry. You were just trying to be helpful."

He smiles and pulls me into a hug.

"It's okay, really," he assures me.

"You want to hang out again?"

He looks at me with a sad expression on his face.

"I do, honestly, but I can't. There's something I need to take care of today. I'm sorry."

"No. It's okay. I get it. You have your own life and all."

He smiles.

"We'll schedule something later, okay?"

He gives me a kiss on the top of my head and gets in his car. I was really hoping we could get together so that I could explain myself. Unfortunately, now my only option is to go home and dwell on it.

Dusty is sleeping in the window when I get there, but quickly gets up and runs over when he hears me get close to the door. He immediately starts meowing at me for food, so the first thing I do before anything else is feed him. Once he's happily eating, I go and plop down on my bed, my brain trying to run through too many thoughts at one time.

I just want my brain to slow down or stop so I can fall asleep, but that doesn't happen. I lie there wide awake, itching to be moving and productive, but somehow also not having the motivation.

Chapter Thirty-Two

The next few days go by in a blur. My headache is subsiding, but my stomach still feels a little funny. I eat with Noah at lunch and everything seems good between us, so that's a plus. I'm back to behaving at work too. All in all, things are going well again. Minus the fact that I'm still not getting sleep.

"Everything's making me mad," I tell Noah on one of our lunch breaks. "I don't get it. I'm just so... frustrated. And I don't even know why."

He takes my hand and gives it a light squeeze.

The rest of our lunch break is spent in silence. I don't want to risk snapping since I'm still crabby. Noah doesn't seem to mind. We watch a stupid video I found on my phone and laugh along with it.

Chapter Thirty-Three

The next few days after that go by without incident. Noah and I go out on another date, this time to see a movie. Work goes smoothly. I know I'm skipping a lot of time here, but really, nothing more exciting has been going on. My headache is better. My stomach is better. That's about it.

Chapter Thirty-Four

It's a couple of weeks before anything notable starts to happen. I feel like I'm starting to see the effect of the medication I'm taking, and I'm not sure I like it. I can't sit still. I'm exhausted, but unable to stay in bed long enough to get actual sleep. I'm stressed. There're a million thoughts fighting in my head for which one should be in the forefront.

On the positive side, I've finally started that baking project I bought all of that stuff for. My kitchen is a mess right now, but I've made three cakes so far, which I've just been giving away, because I'm one person. I can't eat three cakes, or at least, I shouldn't. My decorating skills actually kind of suck, but they taste good, and that's what matters.

I've also been trying again and again to get Dusty used to a harness. I don't think it's going to work.

I've also started working out, painting, jewelry making, and scrapbooking. So far none of these things are panning out, but I feel like there must be *some*thing I can excel at, and I somehow have all of the energy in the world to try new things, so that's what I keep doing. You'd think I'd have crashed by now, but it doesn't feel possible.

Even at work and with Noah, I'm not the same. It's like I can't be upset about anything even if bad stuff happens. I know that part sounds like it should be a really good thing, but I'm smiling and laughing so much it's starting to hurt. Not to mention it probably looks like I'm high as a kite to our visitors.

Sarah seems to like me this way and I get it. It's better to see me too happy than too sad, but I'm starting to think that maybe my doctor is right. I decide to call my mother up one night and ask her about our family history.

"*Hello?*"

"Hi, Mom. It's me, Charlie."

"*Hey, Charlie! How's the new job? How's the apartment? How's life? You don't call your mother enough, you know.*"

"I'm sorry about that. Things are good. My job is good. I don't know if I told you this or not, but I got a cat."

"*You did not!*"

"Sorry about that too, then. Anyway, I actually called with a question."

"*Sure, Hon, what is it?*"

"Well... Um... I was just wondering... do we have any bipolar people in our family?"

"*Why do you ask?*"

Of course she wouldn't just answer the question.

"Because… my doctor thinks that's something I might have."

My mother is quiet for a while on the other end of the phone. At first, I check to make sure she hasn't for some reason hung up on me, but then she finally answers.

"*There is your grandmother on your dad's side. Oh, and one of your aunts on my side. I'm honestly not sure beyond that.*"

"So… you think maybe she could be right?"

Silence again.

"*Well, it is possible. Don't you remember when you were in high school? You've always had these ups and downs. I used to think you were just a moody teenager, but I started to wonder if maybe there might be more to it than that.*"

I take a moment to digest this.

"No," I answer honestly. "I don't remember much at all, really. High school is kind of one big blur in my memory."

"*Well I remember. I know you've been thinking you have depression for a while, Hon, but I think maybe that doesn't explain everything.*"

"But I don't have psychosis. I don't gamble or have frequent unprotected sex. I don't think of myself as being so important and I sure don't have hallucinations."

"*Hon, you can have a disorder without meeting every single one of the criteria. Your dad's mother was*

Bipolar Two, meaning she predominantly experienced depression and suffered from hypomania rather than full-blown mania. There are degrees to this kind of thing. Not everyone with this disorder experiences it the same."

This really isn't the answer that I was hoping for. I'm not sure it comforts me at all. All I can think about is what other people are going to think of me.

She's crazy.

Be careful around her.

She's unstable.

You can't trust her.

And the list goes on.

"Thanks, Mom. I guess this clears some things up for me. I'm gonna have another conversation with my doctor about it when I go to my next appointment."

"*Of course! I love you, Charlie, no matter what. Just remember that.*"

"I love you too, Mom. Bye."

I hang up the phone and lie down on my couch. There's a lot more I need to learn. I go through the list of symptoms online one more time and check all of the ones that apply to me, or have applied to me in the past and occurred at the same time, as the criteria states would be the case.

Depression Symptoms:

Feeling sad, hopeless or irritable most of the time. Check.

Lacking energy. Check.

Difficulty concentrating and remembering things. Check.

Loss of interest in everyday activities. Check.

Feelings of emptiness or worthlessness. Check.

Feelings of guilt and despair. Check.

Feeling pessimistic about everything. Check.

Self-doubt. Check.

Being delusional, hallucinating and disturbed or illogical thinking. No.

Lack of appetite. Check.

Difficulty sleeping. Check.

Waking up early. Not really.

Suicidal thoughts. Check.

Okay, so I definitely fit that side.

Hypo/mania Symptoms:

Feeling very happy, elated or overjoyed. Check.

Talking very quickly. Check.

Feeling full of energy. Check.

Feeling self-important. No.

Feeling full of great new ideas and having important plans. Check.

Being easily distracted. Check.

Being easily irritated or agitated. Check.

Being delusional, hallucinating and disturbed or illogical thinking. Again. No.

Not feeling like sleeping. Check.

Doing things that often have disastrous consequences – such as spending large sums of money on expensive and sometimes unaffordable items. I did once get myself into some pretty bad debt from my overspending, which ruined my credit for a while… Check.

Making decisions or saying things that are out of character and that others see as being risky or harmful. Overspending? Yes. Reckless driving? Yes. Soooo…. Check.

Huh. I guess I do fit it kind of well. And it does run in my family. Maybe I should let my doctor know that the next time I'm there.

For now, I stare up at my ceiling. Dusty comes and lays down on top of my stomach. He's only eleven pounds, but somehow it feels like more. I pet him and can feel the rumbling when he purrs. It's a very soothing feeling.

Somehow, lying here like this, I eventually doze off. It's the first time I've had a nap in a while, and I welcome it with open arms. I don't dream about anything, at least nothing I can remember. When I wake up it's past my usual dinner time, so I make a bowl of cereal and go right back to the couch to watch some TV.

After that I read a book. After that I watch TV again. After that I take a bubble bath. After that I watch TV again. I do everything but go to bed. I decide to text Noah, even though I know he's not likely to get my messages until morning. I'm pretty sure he sleeps like a normal person, after all.

Me: `Hey. I can't sleep. I was wondering if you're awake?`

After twenty minutes of him not answering, I decide that I was right. He must be asleep. I scroll through social media until it's time for me to get up in the morning.

Everything Is Alright

Chapter Thirty-Five

The next time I'm in my doctor's office I tell her about everything I've learned and everything I've been thinking. I'm surprised when she suggests adding another antidepressant to combat the high the other one is giving me. Seems like it would only make the issue worse, but apparently, they're not in the same drug class so it works somehow? I don't know. Don't ask me.

Anyway, I start taking this right away as well. I notice when it starts to really take effect, but I don't think this is the reaction she was hoping for, because instead of lowering my mood to a healthy level I crash. Hard.

-

It's a Wednesday morning when I notice it. My alarm goes off in the morning, but getting up is the last thing I want to do. I shut it off and lie there for a moment before reluctantly pulling myself out of bed. I get dressed slowly. I'm just… not in the mood to go to work today.

When I get there everyone's as cheery as always. I say good morning quietly to them all and get right to work. Sarah comes in a little later than me and I must look tired, because once again she asks:

"Everything okay?"

I nod.

"I'm just tired."

Even getting a little caffeine in my system doesn't do the trick. I'm sluggish the whole day. I vent about it to Noah when we have lunch together.

"I guess I'm just starting to wonder what I would do if no medication works for me."

"Why are you even entertaining that thought? You've only tried two."

"I know, but… I don't know, actually. I guess I was scared even before I started taking anything. It's been a long-time fear of mine, and partially why I've never tried to get help before."

"Look at this this way. You won't know if you don't try," he reminds me.

"True. I suppose I should still give it a shot."

My eyes start to sting and it's not long before they start to water.

"What's wrong?" asks Noah.

I wipe my eyes, trying not to full-on cry.

"I'm just so tired, Noah. I've barely gotten any sleep in a month, and I think it's finally catching up with me. My poor body is giving up."

He pulls me into a hug.

"I didn't realize it was that bad."

I shrug.

"Not like I showed it much. I did everything in my power not to."

"Think you'll be okay for the rest of the day?"

I nod.

"I'll make it. I just don't think I'm gonna be on top of my game today. Might take my time."

"That's okay to do, you know. You don't have to rush through everything all the time."

"I know. I just like getting things done and out of my way so I can relax."

"And sometimes it's okay to relax in the middle," he reminds me.

I know this. I really, truly do. It's just… how I've always been. I get things done and I get them done quickly. I think it's just the way that I was raised. I grew up in a household where you simply didn't put things off. If you were gonna do something, you did it right away.

I think about what Noah said, though, when I go back to the office. I get to work right away, but I take a break after about five minutes just to rest my brain. I'm reading through some online message boards for a few minutes before I go back to tedious data entry. There's a special project we're working on for Erik and this one requires a lot more concentration than what I'm typically used to.

Sarah and I don't talk much. I see her look over in my direction every so often, but she's working on the same project I am, so I guess she needs to focus on that too. It's oddly quiet up front in the admissions office today. Not to mention how we have almost no visitors.

The last few hours of the shift go by slowly. I'm watching the clock the whole time, waiting for it to hit 5:00. I just want to go home and nap, or take a bath, or something. Pet Dusty. Maybe play with him if I feel up to it.

When it finally is time to head home I'm out of my desk the minute the clock lands on the hour. I don't even wait around to see Noah. I just book it to my car and climb inside. Luckily the drive home is short, so I'm there before I know it. Once I get inside I drop my bag on the floor, feed Dusty, and then collapse onto the couch.

Dusty comes over after he's done eating and sniffs at the hand I leave draped over the edge of the couch, then rubs against it, so I reach out a little to try and pet him. It's not long before I fall asleep, though, and when I wake up he's lying on my back.

The clock tells me it's now 8:45 PM and I've slept through my usual dinner time once again. I get up and do the only thing I can do, pour cereal and milk in a bowl and call it good. I think I've been doing this too often lately, but I really don't have it in me to care too much about that.

After I eat I brush my teeth and go straight to bed.

I don't sleep well. I keep waking up and falling back asleep. I don't think I dream about anything. If I do,

I can't remember the dream. Because of this, it feels like I didn't actually get any sleep in those brief moments I was unconscious. Just feels like I've been tossing and turning all night long.

When morning finally comes around I shut my alarm off with a long sigh and pull my phone out. I'm calling off work today. I'm too tired to go. There's a nagging pain in my head, throbbing with each beat of my heart. I get up only to take a painkiller before flopping back into bed and rolling up underneath the covers.

I'm not sure how long it's been before I get a text from Noah.

Noah: Not feeling well today?

Me: No.

Noah: :(I hope you feel better soon.

Me: Thanks. :)

I spend some time playing games on my phone until I eventually decide to try sleeping again. My stomach rumbles, but right now I don't care. I ignore it and bundle up tighter.

I wake up from my nap a few hours later, but I still don't feel like getting out of bed. I do, only to make myself some toast, eat it, go to the bathroom, and then go right back. A few other people have texted me so far this morning, but I ignore them all. Dusty has bundled himself up next to me in bed. He's all the company I need.

I'm just tired. I'm so tired. I don't want to do anything. I don't want to go anywhere. I feel like I haven't slept in a year. Guess all those late nights finally caught up to me. I just hope this feeling doesn't last.

Chapter Thirty-Six

Time's really flying by now that I'm sleeping through most of the day. Tomorrow comes quickly and I take another day off work to do exactly the same. Noah texts me again. Sarah does too this time. I don't answer either one of them back.

How did I end up here? Wasn't I recently so happy I could barely contain it? Now I feel like I'm dragging, like nothing's really worth the effort. My job? Why do I bother? My relationship? Why do I bother? I think about how reassuring Noah is and I try to remind myself of the things he's always telling me, but it doesn't do much for me. Instead I just find myself growing annoyed.

I'm growing annoyed by the simple act of trying to make myself feel better. Like… why? Why can't I just let myself be sad? I'm allowed to be sad. I'm allowed to have a bad day or two. Except, I have to go to work tomorrow regardless. I don't want to take too much time off considering I'm still in my probationary period.

For today's lunch I slap some peanut butter on a slice of bread and that's it. I do fill a water bottle, though, and bring it back to bed to put it on my bedside table. Might as well not dehydrate myself too. I'm already not eating enough.

I'm lying back in bed staring up at the ceiling when my phone rings. I don't want to answer it, but then I see that it's Noah and he almost never actually calls me so I feel like I need to.

"Hello?" I answer.

"*Hey. I'm on lunch right now. Just wanted to check in and see how you're doing.*"

"I'm fine," I lie for the hundredth time.

"*Feeling any better at all?*"

"Honestly, not really. I must have picked up a bug or something." Another lie.

"*Well, I hope you feel better soon. I miss you already.*"

This makes me smile for the first time in the past day and a half.

"I miss you too."

We talk a little longer about work-related things. He fills me in on anything I've missed, information he mostly gets from Sarah. I ask him why she doesn't just tell me herself, but he says he doesn't know, and that maybe she just figures I'd be more willing to talk to him. He has a point. I did ignore her last text. She must assume I don't want to talk to her right now.

She wouldn't be wrong either.

"*Well, I've got to get back to work. See you soon?*"

"Yeah. I'm sure by tomorrow I'll be feeling better."

"*I hope so... see you tomorrow then, maybe.*"

"See you tomorrow."

"*Bye.*"

He hangs up and I put my phone on the table, once again ignoring whatever else has popped up on my lock screen.

I do eventually get bored lying in bed all day, so I migrate out to the couch and find one of the shows I'm currently binge watching. I wrap myself under a throw blanket and hug one of the decorative pillows for comfort. Dusty comes out and goes to his cat tree so he can lie in the sunshine streaming in through the open curtain.

-

Later on in the evening I get up off the couch and find a granola bar in my cupboard and some crackers and call that dinner. I take it back to the couch and snack while watching my show. I've watched six episodes so far and plan to keep going until later tonight. I know that after lying in bed for two days I should really take a bath or a shower or something, but I decide I'm just not up to it.

People don't realize how hard it is to do basic things when you're depressed. It may seem simple to take a bath or make yourself something to eat, but let me tell you, it is not. Most people think of it as "I'm going to take a shower." I think of it as:

1. Turn water on.
2. Wait for it to get warm.
3. Take off clothing.
4. Get in shower
5. Wash my hair.
6. Wash myself.
7. Get out of shower.
8. Dry myself off.
9. Put new clothing on.
10. Brush hair.

It's at least a ten-step process. Ten steps I don't have the energy or motivation to take. Maybe it's weird to break things apart like that in my mind, but that's literally how my brain processes the act of showering. It's not something I just do. It's a process.

Same with making food. Gotta get out dishes, ingredients, cut stuff, cook stuff, plate it, clean dishes after, clean kitchen if need be, stuff like that. Every task becomes a process with steps. How many steps there are depends on what the task is, but they all have steps. All of them. There's no simplicity in it anymore.

So I don't shower. I don't even take a bath, which is easier, because at least I get to sit down. Instead, I change into clean pajamas and consider that good enough. After I'm done watching TV I go back to bed and try to get some legitimate sleep. I toss and turn, though, all night long. I barely even remember closing my eyes at all by the time my alarm goes off.

Chapter Thirty-Seven

Work the next day kind of sucks. I start off my day by getting out of bed and throwing whatever's clean on. After that I grab a granola bar from the cupboard and say good-bye to Dusty, tell him I'll be back as though he actually knows what I'm saying.

When I get to work my coworkers are as cheery as ever. How are they always so cheery this early in the morning. I put a fake smile on my face and pretend that everything's okay.

"Are you feeling better then?" Sarah asks.

"Yes," I say. "I feel fine now."

I don't. Not really. Not completely. I'm still so tired that I order a caffeinated drink from our on-campus coffee shop and pray that it will make things easier for me.

The first part of the day is pretty slow. We're far enough into the semester now that we don't really have a lot to do. There are some students we deal with who are planning to come for winter, and we do still get visitors, but not too many. I prefer when it's busier. The slowness of the morning tempts me to close my eyes for just a minute….

"Hey. Charlie. Sure, you feel okay?"

I jump at the sound of Sarah's voice.

"Uh… yeah. I'm just tired. I hadn't gotten a lot of sleep over the past two nights. But I feel fine. Don't worry about it."

She gives me a look that tells me she knows I'm full of crap.

I ignore her and go about my day. This morning it's mostly helping out with mail, since there's not much else to do and we send a heck of a lot of mail out of our office. I don't mind doing it. Gives me something to do. It's tedious, but I kind of like tedious, especially because right now it makes it easier to focus on this one thing and not all of the things that are bothering me.

And there's a lot bothering me.

I've woken up today feeling less than confident in myself. I don't know why. I haven't done anything wrong yet, but I'm just waiting to screw something up, knowing that I will at some point. Then I start to wonder why I took this job. All these people are happy and normal and I'm… not. I'm not happy right now. I've never been normal.

I know that Sarah and Noah have both told me that everyone has their own issues, but it feels like my issues are worse. I mean, no one else looks like they'd rather be anywhere else right now. Just me.

We fill up seven buckets of mail that I take downstairs on a cart. I hate this cart. It's noisy. It rattles. I feel like I'm the loudest thing in the building every time I have to use it. I grip the handles hard and wince as I push it over tiled floor.

"Noah missed you," Sarah tells me when I get back.

"I know. He texted me."

"Right. Duh. I suppose that's something he would have done… I missed you too."

I smile for the first time today.

"It's good to know I was missed. Makes me feel like people actually want me here."

She gives me an odd look.

"Why would we not want you here?"

I shrug.

"I don't know. I'm so awkward and it takes my brain so long to grasp things and respond to people and I mess stuff up and people have to correct things for me and I just feel like that must not be fun to deal with."

"Charlie. You're new. You have to stop beating yourself up. We all like you here."

Right now, I can't see why, because my brain is spiraling. All of a sudden everything comes flooding into my thoughts at the same time. I'm a screw up. I disappoint people. Nobody actually likes me. They're all just lying. I'm a burden. Nobody wants me here. Etc. I sit at my desk and stare at my computer screen, not knowing what to do.

It takes me a minute to realize what's going on. Clearly my meds are not working. In fact, I think this one my doctor added might be making my depression even worse. I feel like shit right now. I hate everything and everyone. I'm going to have to talk to her, but…

Ugh. I don't want to.

I wait for lunch to come around and then practically fall into Noah's arms when I see him, almost causing him to drop the food container he's holding.

"Woah. Hey there. Everything okay?"

I shake my head.

"Far from it, actually."

"What's going on?"

I tell him about everything I just mentioned.

"Is it possible for a medication to make me feel worse?" I ask when I'm done.

"New or worsening depression is typically labeled as a side effect for a lot of things. I'm sorry to hear that it's so bad right now, though."

"The weekend's coming up and I have to do laundry because that's building up and I have to do the dishes, because those are somehow piling up too, even though I've barely been eating anything."

"Speaking of which," he says. "You didn't bring lunch with you today?"

"Oh… no. I had a granola bar earlier."

"A granola bar is not enough food, Charlie."

"I know…. I know."

He breaks off half of his turkey sandwich and hands it to me.

"You need to eat something."

I take it reluctantly. It's good, though. He didn't put anything gross on it like mustard or something.

"Thanks."

"Not a problem. Do you want me to come over this weekend?" he asks. "I can help you out."

I look up at him, surprised.

"Huh?"

"I can come over if you'd like. This weekend. I'll help you take care of stuff."

"You really don't have to do that," I tell him.

"I know, but I want to if it helps you."

I smile.

"You're sweet, but I couldn't ask you to."

"You don't have to. I'm volunteering."

"Well… okay. I guess."

He smiles and pulls me into a hug.

"We got this," he tells me. "I got you."

Sometimes I really do wonder how I ended up with someone as sweet and kind and funny as Noah. And cute, very cute. Let's not forget that part. Sometimes it seems too good to be true, and the worry that this is all in my imagination starts to seep in again.

I rest my head on his chest and listen to his heart beat. Feel it. Feel him breathing. Feel the warmth he gives off.

He's definitely real.

Everything Is Alright

Chapter Thirty-Eight

Saturday morning Noah shows up bright and early, waking me up earlier than I'd prefer. In fact, he caught me off guard and I am a total mess in my pajamas, with crazy, messed up hair. I rush to get ready as fast as I can before I open the door. At least if anything, he's gotten me out of bed and dressed for the day, so he's already helping.

"I didn't say come here this early," I complain once I open the door.

He just smiles and follows me inside.

He looks cute wearing sweatpants and a t-shirt. It's so unlike how I normally see him that it throws me off for a second.

"So. What do you want to do first?" he asks.

"Umm… laundry I guess."

I'm ashamed to let him see my bedroom, but since most of my laundry is currently scattered about my bedroom floor, I don't have much of a choice. He helps me pick it up and get it into the basket so we can take it downstairs where the laundry room is. Admittedly, this is why I haven't been keeping up with it lately. The whole up and down the stairs thing is exhausting if you're carrying literally anything.

Once all of my laundry is loaded we head back upstairs and go right to my couch.

"I wanna do one thing at a time," I say. "So we're holding off on the dishes."

He nods.

"Okay. That's alright."

I turn on the tv and cuddle up to him.

"Thanks for helping me out. I really do appreciate it."

"Of course."

I set a timer on my phone so we know when to go move my laundry over to the dryer. In the meantime, we watch some random movie that I find.

"Have you eaten anything for breakfast?" I ask.

"Um… no. I woke up and came right over."

"Well, I do still have some clean bowls and stuff if you want cereal. Or I could make toast. Whatever you feel like."

"Cereal is fine."

I let him pick what kind he wants, since I have four different options and, after he's done counting to make sure there's an even number of pieces in his bowl, we go back to the couch. It feels weird to have Noah sitting next to me this early in the morning, in loungewear and eating my cereal. He looks so comfortable and relaxed, while I am anything but.

I'm too aware of him next to me.

Dusty sits on the couch in between us, his head resting against the side of my thigh. I'm honestly surprised he's not trying to eat our cereal. Normally he's pawing at my bowl.

When we're done I bring the bowls over to the sink and add them to the ever-growing pile. I let out a sigh as I look at how big it's gotten. Then I push it out of my head and rejoin Noah on the couch.

We're about a third of the way into the movie when the alarm goes off to signal it's time to move my clothes over. Since I've been so lazy lately, I have another load of laundry that needs to get started as well. Noah carries this load down and I move the other load from the washer to the dryer. He loads the washer for me.

When we get back upstairs I set another alarm and hit play on the movie.

"You look extra cute all casually dressed," I tell him.

He smiles and pulls me close to him.

"Is that so?"

I nod.

"Super cute. Cuter than I thought possible."

He laughs at this.

"You're pretty cute yourself."

I don't feel like it, since I'm wearing leggings and a t-shirt and my hair's been thrown mostly into a small ponytail, but okay. I'll take his word for it.

We watch the movie in silence until the next alarm goes off, and then we move my clothes again. We finish the movie about the same time we finish the laundry, and then it's on to the dreaded dishes.

I don't know what it is about dishes, but there's something about standing there scrubbing and rinsing and drying that's too difficult for me to do on my own. At least lately, that is.

Noah agrees to wash them while I dry and put away. It goes by a lot faster than I expect it to because of our team effort, which is nice.

"So, what do you have planned for tomorrow?" he asks. "Anything?"

"Not really."

"Wanna go out somewhere? It can just be for a walk."

"Oh… um… I guess a walk could be nice. Better than lying around doing nothing, which is honestly what would be the most likely case."

"Great. I'll come by around noon and maybe we can stop to eat somewhere."

"Sounds great."

"So what do we do now?" he asks.

Well, we're officially done with my chores. Technically he doesn't need to be here any longer, but why not have him stay a little while just for fun? I grab his hand and lead him back to my couch.

"We could either watch something, or we could turn something on and act like we're going to actually watch it, but you know… not."

He smiles and follows me over, sitting down next to me.

"I think I like the second option a little more."

-

Later on, in the evening, Noah is still in my apartment. I'm lying with my head on his chest since we've gone back to watching TV. Neither of us wants him to leave, but I feel like this isn't the time to ask him to stay the night. He wouldn't be prepared. It's not like I have clothes he would fit into if he wanted to shower and change into something new. But that means he has to leave, and it's been so nice spending the afternoon cuddling on the couch.

"Thank you again for coming over and helping me out."

"Course. I'm glad to."

"Seriously, though. You're the best."

He gives me a quick kiss and smiles.

"Remember, I get it."

"I know. It's just… it's so hard to believe that I found someone so kind-hearted. It's not what I'm used to when it comes to my mental health. And like, I know that you have your own struggles, and that helps you be more understanding, but for some reason I still find it a little unbelievable."

"I could say the same to you. You held off on starting the movie for me so I could tediously count out pieces of cereal."

"Told you it wouldn't bother me."

"Oh, just wait. It's only the beginning."

I playfully smack his arm.

"I mean it. It's not going to bother me."

"Right. Just… hard to believe and all. Goes both ways."

I smile and wrap my arms around him to give him the biggest hug I am capable of giving.

Chapter Thirty-Nine

As promised, Noah shows up around noon and we go on our walk. There's a little cafe not too far from where I live, so we make that our destination. It's sunny and warm outside, which makes for good walking weather.

"I'm thinking about adopting a dog," Noah tells me.

"Oh really?"

He nods.

"Yeah, I've been thinking about it since you asked me if I had any pets. I miss having one."

"That would be nice. Know what kind you'd get?"

"Anything but those little yippy things," he says with a laugh. "I'm sure they're lovable and I know they deserve homes too, but I can't do all that high-pitched barking."

"I get it."

"I'd love a German shepherd. I used to have one when I was a kid. His name was Oliver. I'd take just about any dog, though."

"We should go look. They're open until 4:00."

"Today?"

"It could be fun," I say in an attempt to persuade him. "You could finally have a dog again. And you can always run home on lunch or breaks to take him out and stuff so you wouldn't have to worry about him being alone the whole day. You could even hire a pet sitter if you wanted."

"What if we *just* look? I'm not sure I'm ready to make a commitment yet."

"That's fine too."

We make it to the cafe and order our food. While we're waiting for it to be brought out, I've already pulled out my phone and looked up our local shelter's website. I go to the dog section and start scrolling through, holding my phone out so Noah can see them too.

"Would you like a puppy or a little older? I ask.

"Little older."

Okay, we have:

Drax, an American Blue Heeler/Mix. Neutered. Male. 3 years, 2 months.

Max, a Terrier, Airedale/Mix - Neutered. Male. 5 years, 3 months.

Nova, a Treeing Walker Coonhound, Black and Tan/Mix. Female. 2 years, 5 months.

Annie, Hound/Retriever, Labrador. Female. 2 years, 11 months.

Chase, Terrier, American Pit Bull/Mix. Neutered. Male. 3 years, 1 month.

"What do you think? I personally like Drax and Nova."

"They're all cute," he says.

"They're all good with respectable children, though that isn't a concern at the moment. A few of them might not work with cats… which could be an issue."

Noah gives me a sly smile.

"You suggesting we're gonna live together at some point?"

Whoops. I didn't even realize how that would sound.

"Well… you already assumed you'd be the father of my future children, so… I just figured."

He laughs.

"Okay. You got me there."

"Only two of them aren't so keen on other dogs," I point out.

"Well, I only plan on adopting one, so that's not an issue."

"So which one do you like?" I ask.

"Well, Nova is good with cats and children. She's only about two and half years old. Young, but not technically a puppy anymore."

"We should go visit her!" I say. "You know, meet her in person."

He thinks it over for a moment.

"Sure. Why not?"

"Yay!"

Once we're done with the cafe we walk back to my apartment and get in Noah's car. I'm excited and my mood definitely feels better than before.

The drive there is mostly quiet. Noah has the radio tuned to some country station, which I don't mind. I'm not a huge country fan, but I do like some of it. In fact, I quietly sing along to one of the songs that I know pretty well. I can see Noah smiling at this out of the corner of my eye. I'm surprised when he doesn't call me out on it.

I'm also surprised when we get there that the lady up front remembers me, but I suppose it hasn't been too long since I adopted Dusty.

"Hi! How can I help you guys today?" she asks.

"He's looking for a dog," I answer before Noah can even open his mouth.

"Oh! Great! Follow me this way."

She gestures toward the door with all the barking on the other side of it, and we follow her over. Once inside, the dogs start going nuts, most jumping at their kennel doors and barking. Noah lets a few of them lick his hand as he walks by. Nova's kennel is second to last. She's a little more timid than the others, but she still comes up to sniff and lick Noah's hand.

"Would you like to take her for a walk?" the woman asks us.

"Yes!" I blurt out before Noah has a chance.

He gives the woman a smile that I know melts her heart just a little bit.

"Yes, we would like that."

We watch as she opens the kennel and goes inside, putting a leash on Nova before walking her out to us. Nova eagerly wags her tail as the woman hands Noah the leash. There's a large fenced off yard out back that she leads us to.

Nova's happy to be outside. She's sniffing everything in sight. She only pulls a little as Noah tries not to let her get too far ahead of us.

"Noah and Nova. That may get confusing," I say as we walk.

"Huh. I hadn't even noticed."

"Neither did I until just now. Maybe that means she's perfect for you, though."

He looks down at her and smiles.

"She does seem like a nice dog."

"You should adopt her."

"Charlie, I am not prepared for a dog in the least right now."

"So, we can prepare you. All we need to do is a little shopping."

I can tell he thinks I'm a little crazy, but there is also a part of him that's actually considering it. I can tell by the way that he looks at her, like he'll be sad if she gets adopted by someone else before he can fully prepare himself.

So, he agrees to adopt her.

"Yes!"

He laughs.

"You know, I'm not sure whether or not you're a good or bad influence on me. I find myself living a little more impulsively than I typically would."

"I say it's a good influence. Everyone deserves a little spontaneity in their life from time to time."

He shakes his head, but he's still got a smile on his face that tells me at least a small part of him agrees with me.

The shelter lady is happy when we walk back in and announce that we, well, he will be adopting Nova today. She gets all of the paperwork ready. As Noah fills it all out and signs off on it, I make a mental list of things that we'll need for him to be prepared.

Leash, which I guess they're letting us keep.

Food.

Food and water dishes.

A bed.

A brush.

Toys.

Treats.

When we get Nova into the car she wants to be up front with us and tries climbing in between our seats. I spend the ride trying to keep her in the back while Noah drives. Once we get to the store I give him the list and wait in the car with Nova while he does the shopping.

He comes back to the car with a shopping cart full of bags and the dog's bed. After loading it all into the back, he climbs back in the driver's seat.

"I still can't believe you talked me into this," he says, but he does so with a smile on his face.

"I mean, you already knew you wanted a dog."

"Yeah, I just didn't think I would be going home with one *today*."

Noah drives me back to my apartment and drops me off. I say good-bye to him and Nova before rushing upstairs and collapsing onto my couch. It's been a long weekend.

Everything Is Alright

Chapter Forty

Spending the weekend with Noah did make me feel better, but once he's gone I'm right back to where I started. My general mood is down. My confidence is still low. I go into Monday morning not feeling any better than I did when I left last week. It heightens my anxiety every time someone calls or walks into our office. It's like I'm afraid of messing everything up all of a sudden.

Worrying about messing up actually makes me mess up. Not too bad. Not bad enough for me to freak out like I did last time, but I'm growing more and more frustrated with myself as the day goes on. It's just a bunch of stupid little mistakes here and there. I think Sarah can tell I'm off my game by the way she keeps looking at me. She looks concerned. I tell her about my weekend with Noah, though, and about Nova. She likes that. She has a dog herself.

-

From here on out things get significantly harder. I think there's something about a new job and a new apartment and a new relationship and a new cat that was simply keeping me in a sort of high. Now, all of that is wearing off. My high is gone. I'm reverting back to my depressive state.

And it sucks.

I don't know how to accurately convey depression in terms someone without it would understand. I'm not so good with that kind of thing, but it's basically all consuming. A dark cloud is always over my head, following me wherever I go. That probably sounds pathetically cliché the way I put it, but that's what it is. I'm always sort of in this darkness.

It's a suffocating darkness. Sometimes the pain feels physical even when I know it's in my head. I struggle with that the most. That feeling. I'd never wish it on anyone, no matter how much I disliked them.

I'm watching the minutes tick by on the clock, one after the other. There are still two hours left of my Monday, and I'm already mentally ready to be done with it. I just want to go home and take a nap or something. I slept last night, decently even, and I'm still tired.

I think that's the part that's the hardest to explain to people. The part where mental illnesses can feel, and sometimes actually be, pretty physical too. It's a concept a lot of people in my life have failed to grasp, which is why I constantly get told "you're too young to have 'insert problem here.'"

NMFoster19: How are you holding up today?

CECooper26: Crappy.

NMFoster19: 😟

CECooper26: I’m just having a rough day. I want to get home and nap or something. Don’t worry about me.

NMFoster19: Not gonna lie, kinda hard not to when “crappy” is your response.

CECooper26: It’s just one crappy day.

Except it isn’t just one crappy day.

The day after that is crappy too.

And the day after that.

And the day after that.

And so on…

Playing with Dusty and keeping my apartment at some level of clean (for Dusty’s sake) is about as good as life gets. Other than that, I’m barely keeping up with laundry. My dishes are piling up again. I haven’t taken a shower or a bath in days. Brushing my teeth feels like torture. I opt for comfortable clothing at work, because I can’t stand to put in the effort to go for cute.

Noah notices of course, but he doesn’t say much. I think he just doesn’t know *what* to say.

“You need any help with anything?” he asks.

"No," I lie, because it's easier than making him come help me again.

For some reason I don't want to do that. He's my boyfriend, not my personal caretaker. He shouldn't be coming over to help clean for me all the time. Not that I've let him aside from that one weekend.

"Have you talked to your doctor?" he asks.

"No. Not yet."

I keep meaning to, but somehow it keeps getting put off.

"Charlie."

"I know. I know. I will. I promise."

Except I don't, and things keep getting worse. I'm clearly suffering from a depressive episode, but the problem with depression is that it makes doing things to get out of that episode difficult. I know what I should be doing. I want to do it. But I don't.

I know what you're probably thinking. How could things get *that* much worse? Or maybe not, but I'm going to explain it anyway, so hear me out.

Chapter Forty-One

I don't know how long it's been. Days. Weeks. I'm not entirely paying attention anymore. Everything sort of blurs together. Dusty, Noah, and work are the only things keeping me from living in my bed. Seriously. I otherwise would. I hate this.

"I can't take it anymore," I say.

"*What do you mean?*" asks Noah, his voice quiet on the other end of the phone call.

"I mean living the way I'm living. I don't want to do anything anymore. I don't feel confident anymore. Everything just sucks."

"*I can come over if you want?*"

It's Saturday again. Dusty and I are both lying on the couch in front of the tv. I'm still in my pajamas.

"No. It's okay. I'll be fine on my own."

"*Are you sure?*"

"Yes. I'm sure. Don't worry about me."

"*Okay.*"

I know he's going to worry about me anyway. I would worry about me if I was him.

Everything Is Alright

-

God, it feels like I'm never going to be happy again. What happened? How did I fall this fast? Or has it not been that fast? I don't remember when this started. I don't actually remember how long it's been. You know why? Because I've hit a point where it feels like this is just how I've always been, and that's not entirely wrong.

If there's one thing I remember most from the last sixteen years it's the depression. There are vague memories of times when I was… something else. The depression is more overwhelming, though. It's like… drowning out all the times that I wasn't. And there were times I wasn't. Deep down I know that.

So why, right now, does it feel like I'm wrong? Why does it feel like those happier memories are false memories? Maybe they were just blinks in time in the midst of being depressed. Insignificant.

-

Remember how I said work is one of the only things keeping me from living in my bed? Well, it's true. I don't want to call in. I don't want to take time off. It's helpful to have something to do. It's helpful to feel like I have a purpose for eight hours a day five days a week. I help people. I like that I help people. Plus, there are other people to talk to, which means I'm not alone in my own head so much. Honestly, my job keeps me sane to a degree. People wonder why I don't take more days off if I'm not feeling well, but that's honestly why.

I mean, look at things this way…

I live alone with my cat. I have a job that I like but it pays me shit. I have an old car that honestly could break down at any moment. I barely scraped by in school, which is partly why I couldn't get a much better job even if I wanted to. I have Noah, but I don't want to bank on having him forever, not with all the problems I've got.

So, what am I living for?

I'm not married. I don't have kids or grandkids. I'm not capable of fixing our climate or ending world hunger. I barely make a difference in anyone's life. I'm not even one of the people that decides who gets into this school, so I can't say I help people *that* much at work either. I don't really have close friends outside of work friends, because they all moved away, and that's just not the same.

I feel like I do the same things every day. I go to work. I come home and watch TV or play with Dusty, and very occasionally these days hang out with Noah. Otherwise I'm basically just… existing. Work takes up most of my waking hours, and I know it's like that for most people in this country, but it's still depressing to think that's about all I ever do. Go to work and go home. And repeat.

I know, I know, I'm sort of throwing a pity party here, but it honestly feels like I don't have a lot to live for. Like… if I wasn't alive it wouldn't really make a difference, ya know?

I'm tired. I'm just… tired.

I have nothing else to say.

-

There's a brief light in my life when Noah asks if he can come over the next weekend. We spend the majority of the time cuddled up on my couch. He brings Nova over to meet Dusty and they seem to get along well enough. No fighting is happening, though Dusty seems a little hesitant to be anywhere too close to Nova.

"Are you sure you don't want me to help you?" Noah asks.

Admittedly, I've let him into my apartment knowing full well that I once again have dirty dishes and laundry lying around. Normally, I wouldn't let anyone see my place like this, but I somehow feel comfortable enough to not worry about scaring Noah off with a little messiness.

"I'm sure."

"Okay. Because you know I don't mind helping."

I roll my eyes.

"Yes. I do know that. I also know that you're my boyfriend, not my personal servant. I believe we've already discussed that before."

He lets out a short laugh.

"I don't know, though. Depends what kind of personal servant we're talking about. I could be into that."

"Oh, my God."

He laughs a little more and pulls me close to him, holding me in his arms.

"I'm joking… Mostly."

I turn to look up at him and find his green eyes burning holes into my own. I can't take it when he looks at me like that, especially this close.

"You are really something else," I say, doing my best to roll over so that he's no longer behind me and we're face to face.

He smiles.

"Oh, I know. I like to think that's part of my charm."

"It is," I admit. "I'll give you that."

This is the easy part of my life. This is the part I wish I could hold onto all the time. Noah is a light in my life shining through all of the darkness. He can't wash it out completely, and I would never expect him to, but he helps.

"So…."

"Yes?" I ask.

"I don't know. I was going to say something, but I lost my train of thought."

"Oh?"

He nods.

"Sometimes when you look at me that happens."

I laugh, because that's how it is for me too. I never thought it would be an issue for him, though.

Sometimes I need to remind myself that I'm not the only one feeling what I'm feeling, especially in regards to this relationship. I have somewhat of the same effect on Noah that he has on me. It's hard to think of someone looking at me that way, though, even after all this time together.

-

Despite me arguing that I don't want him to, Noah pushes me until I finally agree to clean up a little, and agree to let him help. Though he didn't have to push me too hard. Deep down I really did want to do it.

"You'll feel better. Trust me."

I sigh and roll my eyes.

"*Fine*."

Much like last weekend, we do my laundry and my dishes. Noah's right, too. Seeing these two things done does make me feel better. I guess I shouldn't be surprised. He's right a lot.

-

Noah leaves later in the evening, taking Nova with him. Dusty seems to relax more, but I'm going to miss her a little bit. Maybe one of these times I'll have to go to Noah's place to see her. That's a strange thought. Me going to his place. I've tried to imagine what it's like, but I suppose I'll never know until he invites me. I wonder if he will ever invite me.

Chapter Forty-Two

I finally hit a low point that I'm not sure I can come back from. Every time I'm left alone I spiral. I can't be on my own. Living alone, even with my cat, is not going well. Maybe I'm not meant to. That's what it feels like. Every time I'm alone I spiral a little more until I don't know what to do anymore. Even Noah and Sarah are having a hard time trying to cheer me up and keep me going.

Eventually, my light in the dark goes out.

-

It's a few weeks later. I've started neglecting my apartment again and Noah's been trying his best to help me take care of it. I'm just so done, though. I'm done.

"I said no!" I yell at him. "Stop trying so hard. Just… stop. Please."

"Charlie….

"No. No arguing. I've had enough. Sometimes I'm too tired and I don't care if you help me. It's still so tiring and I'm not having it anymore. Not right now."

"You always feel better."

"I said no arguing! Just leave, okay? Leave me alone."

"Charlie, please…."

"Leave, Noah. Now."

Noah leaves my apartment and I go curl up in a cocoon of blankets in my bed. I stay here for hours. I'm crying now, because I yelled at him. I'm crying even though I'm still mad at him.

-

I snap at Sarah at work. I avoid eating lunch with Noah. I take my breaks in a secluded area where I don't have to be around other people. I know this sounds counterproductive, since I just said I shouldn't be left alone, but who am I if not a hypocrite?

Noah texts me and I ignore those too. I ignore his phone calls. When he comes into our office I get up from my desk and pretend I have something else to do in our mail room before he even has a chance to say a word to me. Sarah keeps asking me about it, but I ignore her too. It's none of her business.

I go through the rest of my day on autopilot. I'm just going through the motions. Doing what needs to be done. It's like the world around me doesn't exist. I'm not attached to it right now. I'm simply floating in an abyss of my own, out of touch with reality.

Have I mentioned I'm tired? Probably like eighty times now, huh? It's true is all. I am.

I think about everything for the remainder of the day. How over it all I am. It seems like there's really only one way out. One way to end my suffering. One way to never have to deal with med changes and side effects again. To avoid being a burden to those around me. To stop their worrying. There is one way to get out of all of it, and by the end of the day I've made up my mind.

-

After work I finally call Noah back. He answers on the first ring.

"Hello?"

"Hey. It's me."

"Charlie. I've been worried about you."

I pause as I put the key into the ignition and start my car. I turn on the Bluetooth and let my phone call switch over to the car speakers so I can continue to talk to Noah hands free. When I pull out of the parking lot, I don't take the turn I normally would to go home.

"I'm sorry you've been worried about me. I've just been too tired to talk. You don't have to keep worrying about me anymore, though."

"Are you feeling better?"

"I will be," I answer, though I know it's technically a lie.

"Where are you right now? Are you home yet?"

I can feel the tears welling up in my eyes and wipe them away while I drive.

"No… I've decided to go for a drive."

"Are you sure you're going to be okay?" I sniffle and he must hear it. *"Are you crying?"* he asks.

"It's okay. I'm telling you, you don't need to worry about me anymore. I'm gonna be fine. You just have to trust me."

"Where are you going, Charlie?"

As I drive through the city, I don't want to answer this question. I don't want him to come stop me.

"I told you. For a drive. I… uh… I need to clear my head."

"You sound upset," he points out. *"You shouldn't be driving around if you're that upset. Please just go home. I'll come over. We can talk."*

I sniffle again. My eyes sting from the effort of trying not to cry out loud.

"I don't want to talk, Noah. I just want everyone to stop worrying about me. I want to stop feeling tired. I want to get rid of the pain, because right now everything hurts and I just don't know what else to do."

"You're really starting to worry me, Charlie. Please, just go home."

It takes everything in me not to pull over my car and completely break down. I grip the steering wheel with both hands and squeeze hard.

No. He's right. I should go home. I need to feed Dusty. I don't want to leave him alone and hungry, wondering when he's gonna eat again. Someone will come for me and find him, but that could take a while. I need to make sure he'll be okay first.

I've changed my mind.

I'll go home.

Maybe that's the better option anyway.

"Okay. Fine. I'm going home. But I don't want you to come over. I don't want to talk. I just want to be alone."

"Okay… if you're sure."

"I'm sure."

"Talk later?"

I don't know how to answer him honestly. He'll come over for sure.

"Yeah. Sure." There's a long pause where neither of us says anything. It's at this moment I decide there's something he needs to know. I need to say the words floating around in my head. Now is the best time. "I love you, Noah, but I have to go now, alright? I'm sorry. I really do love you, though. I just think you should know that."

Silence.

"I-"

I hang up the phone, cutting him off. I don't want to hear him say it.

-

When I finally arrive home, I'm greeted by Dusty begging for his food. I fill his bowl for him, and then pick him up to give him a hug before setting him back down in front of his food bowl. Once he's eating I go into my bedroom and shut the door.

I can do this.

It'll all be over soon.

No one will have to worry about me anymore.

I'll no longer be a bother to them.

All of my pain will end.

I keep telling myself these things as I grab the pill bottles from my bag and dump a bunch of each into one hand. I then go into the bathroom and fill a small cup with water.

I can do this.

I throw a bunch of the pills into my mouth. Then I take one last look at myself in the mirror as I bring the cup of water to my mouth. I can literally see the pain, the dark circles under my red eyes and the hollow look in them. I also see a young woman, though. A young woman who still has so much of her life ahead of her. I hear Dusty pawing at my bedroom door and look back down at my hand.

My hand is shaking. The door is shaking too as Dusty continues to paw at it, as if he knows I'm in trouble and he desperately wants in to save me. He shouldn't even be done eating yet. Why is he doing this?

No. I can't do it.

I spit them out into the sink. It leaves a bitter taste in my mouth since they had begun to dissolve. I use the water in the cup to try and rinse my mouth out. I then sit down on my bathroom floor and finally let myself actually cry. I'm like this for five minutes when I hear knocking on my front door.

Noah: It's me. Are you home yet?

Me: Yeah. You can come in. I didn't lock it.

I think a part of me knew that he would show up anyway.

I'm still curled up in a ball on the floor when Noah comes bursting into the bathroom. He looks at the pill bottles on the floor next to me and the pills in the sink. I can see the immediate panic in his eyes.

And he's not alone. Sarah follows shortly behind him and I see her eyes go big.

"Charlie!" is all she says.

"It's okay," I assure them both. "I didn't actually swallow any."

Noah sighs with relief and sits down next to me. Admittedly, it's a little hard to fit three people in this space. We're crammed together, even though Sarah stays standing.

"I'm really glad to hear that."

"I couldn't do it," I say. "Not with Dusty out there needing me. I'm so sorry. I can't believe I even considered it."

He wraps me in a hug and holds onto me.

"It's okay. I'm just glad you're safe."

"About what I said…."

"I love you too," he tells me before I can finish my sentence.

I smile, even though I'm crying, and lean into him. His arms tighten around me. I'm not sure how long we stay like that. Sarah stays standing there looking down at us the whole time. She doesn't say anything or move from her spot.

-

Eventually, we get up off the bathroom floor and head to the living room.

"Thank you for coming here," I say.

We spend the rest of the night watching TV, only this time Noah doesn't leave. He follows me to bed and holds me in his arms while I sleep. Sarah stays out on the couch. For just a small amount of time, everything is okay in the world again.

"What are you thinking?" Noah asks me.

"I need help. More than I'm getting. I can't do this on my own anymore."

"And that's perfectly okay."

Chapter Forty-Three

I decide to voluntarily commit myself to inpatient treatment the next day. It's scary, but I'm so low that I'm more afraid of what will happen if I don't. Noah and Sarah both agree that it's probably a good idea for me. Just means I'm also going to have to work with HR at the university, because even though my probation period has ended, there are still rules to how much time you take off at once, and I really don't want to mess anything up in that regard.

It's not so bad here after you get through all the paperwork and questioning, which there is admittedly a lot of. The days are structured. We're expected to go to bed at a reasonable hour and get at least eight hours of sleep. Because of this, one of the new medications the doctor put me on is an antipsychotic that a lot of people tend to take off label to help with sleep. She also told me it could help if I do have Bipolar Disorder.

I get a little time in the morning to get ready for the day before getting my vitals checked and going through a daily assessment. After that I go to breakfast. After breakfast I usually go on a walk. You can do other things, but I prefer to move around a bit. They have activities for us, quiet time, lunch, dinner, and snacks.

I have a roommate. Her name is Jessica and she's twenty-five years old. I don't mind her. She's nice enough, and we talk sometimes, though she is on the quieter side. We tend to stick together when we do activities. I wouldn't call her a friend, but she's the person I'm closest to in here.

"How long have you been here?" I can't help but ask her one day as we're working on an art project.

"About two months I think. I've sort of lost track of time."

At this point I've only been here for a few days.

"Did you have a roommate before me?"

"Yes. A while back. I'd been on my own for a while when you showed up."

"Oh… sorry."

She shrugs.

"It's okay. I kinda like having someone else around. It gets lonely otherwise."

I smile, because I agree with her.

I'm not sure what exactly landed Jessica in here. I'm not sure what anyone was committed for. I get the feeling it's a rude thing to ask. I suppose people will volunteer that information if they feel like it. I assume this because no one's asked me, which I'm totally okay with. I'm still not one-hundred percent sure what's wrong with me. I only have a "maybe" diagnosis.

Jessica seems pretty intently focused on her art project, so I take a moment to look at the other patients in the room. There's a guy sitting in the corner by himself, rocking back and forth. There's a large red-headed lady that likes to talk to everyone, and is considerably louder in volume as well. There are two people who look like they were pulled in off the street, still in their dirty clothing. And there's another older man who's currently caught up in the red-headed lady's whirlwind of words.

Next, I look at the room itself. It's rather plain in here. There's the odd painting on the wall in a few spots, but it's otherwise pretty bleak. Everything's gray and cold. I'm not sure how this is an environment meant to help heal people.

I get done with my project and head back to my room early. I'm not sure what else to do. Jessica has pretty much been the only person I talk to, aside from occasionally the red-headed woman. My social anxiety prevents me from trying to converse with anyone else.

I lie on my simple bed looking up at the ceiling and take a moment to reflect on how I got here. I remember crying on the floor with Noah. I remember holding a bunch of pills in my hand. I remember them ending up in the sink, a bitter taste in my mouth. Honestly, though, the whole experience is a little bit of a blur. I think my brain's trying to push it to the dark corners in the back of my mind, never to be seen again.

Speaking of these simple beds, they're not very comfortable. They're pretty stiff. I'm glad they started me on a new med to help me sleep, because there is no way I'd be sleeping here otherwise. I miss my fluffy bed with way too many decorative pillows and a thick comforter. I hope I start doing better soon, because I already can't wait to get out of here.

I do think this new medication is kicking in much faster than the antidepressants I'm still taking. I already feel a little happier. I'm able to get out of bed and go to meals and occasionally watch tv or participate in activities. Am I all better? No. But I'm getting there.

Taking care of myself is still hard. Showering is the literal worst. I do it, but I hate every second of it. Every single second. It's torture is what it is. I don't know why, but that's the truth. It just sucks.

"Dinner's gonna be soon," Jessica says from the doorway. I prop myself up to look at her. "I thought you'd want to know."

"Thank you."

I didn't realize I'd been lying in bed so long. It felt like it had only been a couple minutes. I feel like I just blinked, closed my eyes for a second, and suddenly it was almost dinner. How had that happened?

I get up and go to the cafeteria with everyone else. There are a lot more people here now, more than we had during our art session. The circle tables are almost full. I take my spot next to Jessica who's talking to the red-headed woman. I don't join their conversation, just sit and listen.

"I'm telling you, the red-headed woman says. (Her name turns out to be Carol.) "I know what I saw."

"Carol, there are no aliens or whatever you think you saw in the ceiling," says Jessica.

"But I saw its glowing eye. It was looking right at me."

"That was a smoke detector. There's a light on it to let you know if the battery is dying or not."

"It was red, though," Carol argues, "and you know what that means."

"No, actually, I don't. Why don't you enlighten me?"

"It means they're mad."

Jessica rolls her eyes.

"Carol, I promise you, there are no aliens in the ceiling that are watching us at night."

Carol huffs.

"Sure there are. I saw one. And right after I saw it the whole room turned red. I think they figured me out and called for backup."

"That was tail lights on a car."

Carol shakes her head.

"You'll see," she says. "They'll come for you next."

Carol goes back to eating only for a moment before she starts talking again, ignoring her food. All I can think about is the fact that it's getting cold. My mind isn't even focused on the alien conversation, which is much more interesting than someone letting their food get cold.

"There are probably more," she says. "In all the ceilings. I'd be scared if I were you. You don't know why they're there. They could be plotting something."

I tune out the rest of their conversation and focus on eating. I'm taking small bites of everything. Usually when I'm in a low mood I don't even have the energy to eat food. I'm starving, though, so I force it. Most of the food threatens to come back up.

"Are you married?" Carol asks.

It takes a minute for me to realize I'm the one she's asking.

"Huh? Oh. No. I have a boyfriend, though."

"Ah. I have a boyfriend too, but we're supposed to be getting married next year. I guess that actually makes him my fiancé."

"Cool."

I have no idea what else to say back to that.

"What's yours like?"

I smile thinking about Noah.

"He's really sweet," I tell her. "He's a good guy."

"That's good." She smiles at me, then turns back to Jessica. "Jessica doesn't have a boyfriend. She's gay."

"Carol!" Jessica calls out. "You shouldn't just go around telling people that. It's not your information to tell."

"But it's true."

"Maybe I don't want everyone to know."

"I don't mind," I tell her. "I mean it's not a problem or anything."

Jessica sighs.

"I'm glad to hear that. I'm sorry Carol over here doesn't have much of a filter."

"Neither do I when I get in the right headspace for it," I admit. "I always tell people I barely know really personal things."

"Like what?"

"Well… I'm not going to *now*."

Jessica's shoulders slump.

"Ah well. It was worth a shot."

Everything Is Alright

Chapter Forty-Four

I have my first ever therapy appointment the next day. I'm meeting with Dr. Ruby, who I hear is pretty good. A lot of the patients seem to like her. She's a small woman, no bigger than me, with dark brown hair that's pulled back into a neat bun.

"Hi," she says as I walk into the room.

"Hi."

"Is there anything in particular you would like to talk about today?"

"Not really."

"Okay. Let's go over why you're here then. Your depressive episode, yes?"

I nod.

"I almost tried to kill myself," I admit. "Almost OD'ed."

"What stopped you?"

"My cat."

"That's good. I'm glad that you're still here with us today."

She doesn't even know me. She wouldn't have any reason to be glad. Heck, she wouldn't have known if I died. I don't say anything like that, though.

"I'm still feeling a bit down."

"Are you feeling *any* better than you were before?"

"Yes. A little."

"That's good."

"It is."

"Do you still want to kill yourself?"

"I don't know...""

"You don't know."

I shrug.

"No. I don't know. I mean... a part of me doesn't want to. But another part of me says I'm still too overwhelmed with life."

"Why are you overwhelmed with life?"

"A lot of things have changed recently. I got my own apartment. I got a new job. I got a boyfriend. I got a cat. And because my meds weren't working it just became too much to deal with. I felt like I was losing control of it all I guess."

"Does that scare you? Not having control over everything?"

I shrug again.

"I don't know. I guess."

"And do you know why that is?"

"Because... being in control feels safer."

"How so?"

"Well… it's better than being out of control is it not?"

"It can be."

"When is being out of control ever a good thing?" I ask.

"It's more freeing, not needing to have control all the time. It's also less stressful. Sometimes we need to let our lives flow how they're meant to flow."

"Great… but when you have a mental illness that's harder than normal."

"It is."

I wait for her to say more, but she doesn't.

"So, like… yeah. I don't know. It's not all my fault."

"I'm not saying any of it is your fault, Charlie."

"Kinda sounded like it for a minute."

She smiles.

"I'm sorry. I didn't mean to make it sound that way."

We talk about a lot of other things. She asks about my family, my job, living on my own, and my relationship with Noah. We talk about my insecurities. We talk about my fears. The appointment altogether feels super long, but when I check the clock once I get out it is only five minutes past a full hour.

I feel kind of better afterward, which is something I didn't expect. I didn't expect there to be this feeling of a weight being lifted off me just because I sat down and talked to someone a little bit. Maybe therapy is for me after all.

-

Speaking of my family, they don't know that I'm here. No one comes to visit me during visiting hours. Noah would like to, but they only let family. I at least call him when I get the chance. He had called here once to give me his number since I didn't have it memorized. Though finding the phone free is sometimes hard in this place. There are a few people who seem to be on it all the time.

"How are you?" he asks me one day when I finally get the phone.

"I'm alright. A little better. It's still a struggle, but I met with the therapist recently and that actually kind of helped."

"I'm really glad to hear that."

"How are you? How's work? What's the outside world like?"

He laughs. It's a sound I miss hearing. I can picture the smile on his face and I miss that too.

"I'm good. Works going well, minus not being able to see you. The outside world is weird and complex and as good as usual. Dusty misses you."

"Thank you so much for taking care of him for me," I say. "I miss both of you."

"I miss you too. Do you know how long you'll be there yet?"

"I don't. Could be a few more days, could be a few weeks. Depends on how quickly I start doing better I guess." Another woman, one I can't say I've seen too much in my time here, comes up and stands behind me, waiting for the phone. "Okay, I should probably go now. I don't want to hold up the phone too long. Just wanted to see how you were doing."

"Aww. Okay."

"I love you," I say.

"I love you too."

"Bye."

"Goodbye."

I hang up and the woman behind me rushes for the phone, grabs it like it's a lifeline. I go back to my room to find Jessica curled up in bed.

"Everything okay?" I ask.

It's a stupid question. She looks upset. I think I hear her sniffling.

"Yeah," she answers. "It's just… my family isn't going to make it to visitation and they haven't the past few times and it's just been a while since I've seen them. They don't even really answer when I call most of the time. It just goes to voicemail. I leave messages, but they don't call back."

I feel bad for her. If my family knew I was here and didn't visit or call I would be upset too.

"I'm sorry," I say.

"Eh… it's not your fault."

"Still."

She sniffles some more.

"You wanna know why I'm in here?" she asks.

I have been curious.

"Sure."

"I had a psychotic break. It was bad. I was on vacation with my family and I totally lost it. I said some things I shouldn't have. I blamed them for a lot of things. I don't really blame them for not wanting anything to do with me, but it still sucks."

"What do you mean by psychotic break, if you don't mind me asking?"

"Well… I was crying and screaming at them because I was super paranoid they were all against me. I couldn't think clearly at all. My brain was just all over the place. I couldn't tell the difference between fantasy and reality anymore. My anxiety was really bad. It was a lot of things. I was violent, lashing out."

"Is there anything in particular that triggered it?"

She shrugs.

"I don't know. It feels like it just happened. And worst of all, I stayed in that state for about a week. I don't really remember anything about that week, but this is what my family told me once I was somewhat grounded again. That was actually the last time they spoke to me."

"That sounds terrible."

"It is. I lost a whole chunk of time and I didn't know I was destroying my relationship with my family until after it was over."

I can't even imagine what that would be like. Thankfully my doctor told me that Bipolar 2 individuals don't get full psychotic episodes. (Though that doesn't mean Bipolar 2 is the less bad one, trust me.) I never want to experience something like that.

Jessica and I talk a little longer before it's time to go watch a movie. We get to do that sometimes. They don't have the most interesting selection of movies in my personal opinion, but it's something to do. It's a distraction. Most of the patients go to them.

Whoever picked the movie picked a sappy rom-com. I don't mind them, but it makes me think of Noah and that makes me miss him even more. I hope I'm not in here too long.

Everything Is Alright

Chapter Forty-Five

A few days later I think I'm really starting to feel the effects of the new medication. I'm able to get out of bed easier and take a shower. That's the big thing. I can take a shower and it's not torture. In fact, the warm water feels really good on my bare skin. I almost don't want to get out, but I have to, obviously.

I go to breakfast and sit down with Jessica. Today, someone new has joined us. Her name is Armani and she looks younger, probably around nineteen/twenty years old. She's sort of balled up in her chair, arms around her legs, not talking to anyone.

"This is Carol's new roommate," Jessica tells me. "She just got here earlier this morning."

I feel bad for this girl. She looks terrified. She keeps glancing around the room like someone might attack her at any moment. Some of the louder patients seem to be bothering her the most, though I don't blame her for that. They bother me too. There's a guy yelling about something indecipherable in the back of the room.

Today we have eggs and toast, along with some cinnamon dessert thing that looks like a cross between cake and pie. Oh, and orange juice, coffee or water. The orange juice isn't terrible, but it does taste a little watered down. I always pick it anyway, just because it's better than plain water. I'm not good about drinking water, admittedly.

"Where are you from?" I ask Armani.

She doesn't answer.

"She's not one to talk," Jessica tells me.

"Oh. Okay."

Must be tough rooming with Carol.

We eat in a sort of awkward silence. Jessica and I do anyway. Armani stays balled up, not touching the tray in front of her. She looks like she would rather be anywhere else. Honestly, though? Same. I'm feeling better enough that I'm starting to think I don't need to be here anymore, but they want to make sure this isn't just a false breakthrough.

"What's her problem?" a tall skinny man named Asher asks as he sits down at our table. He's pointing at Armani. And I'm pretty sure you aren't supposed to ask that. It's kind of rude.

"Shut up, Asher," Carol says from the next table over. "Mind your own damn business."

He huffs and then stabs his spork into his eggs. He's upset her, though, so now Armani gets up from the table and rushes from the room.

"She not gonna eat that then?" Asher asks, pointing at her food.

Jessica ignores him, so I do too. Asher takes this as a yes and starts scooping her eggs onto his own tray.

When breakfast is over we have a little free time to do whatever we want. I go lie in my bed and stare up at the ceiling again. I guess this is something that hasn't changed yet. I do spend a fair amount of my time lying in bed and staring at the ceiling. I just… I don't know. I wish I had told my family I was here. Then they could come visit me. I don't know any of their numbers, though, I'm too used to them being programmed into my phone.

I walked by the phone earlier, but it was already occupied. They do have books in here. I suppose I could go read for a while. Do I feel like it, though? Not really. Trying to read a book sounds like a good way for me to accidentally fall asleep. Normally I would love to read, but my head isn't there today. Maybe tomorrow.

This is just like when I was a teenager in high school, though. I used to lie in bed all the time then too, when I wasn't in school that is. Of course, at that time I would plug some earbuds into my phone and listen to music while playing solitaire. I can't have my phone here, so that's not an option.

It really makes me think of being a teenager again. I remember all the things I did that I never thought had anything to do with mental illness. I hadn't started overspending yet, because I didn't have a job, and therefore had no money, but I did engage in some risky behavior.

I snuck out at night to hang with friends and sometimes lied about what we were doing even when my parents *did* know I was going out.

I talked to strangers online that I knew were at least twice my age.

I thought I was hot shit sometimes, and that I deserved to have everyone's attention, so much so that I spread rumors about myself.

I functioned on a few hours of sleep.

I jumped from one hobby to the next.

I was loud and couldn't sit still and my brain was always racing.

I wore inappropriate clothing to school.

How had I not realized these things before? And oh, my God I'm ashamed of most of them. Okay… all of them. I know, some of that may seem like normal teenage crap, but like… all of it at the same time? And I felt so good? Even though I supposedly had depression? I don't know…

I was a little bit like that into college as well. During hyposexuality I sent risqué pictures of myself to some random guys through Snapchat. And, like I mentioned before, I also destroyed my credit. I've gotten several speeding tickets. I did dumb things people dared me to do and almost got us kicked out of a few places.

I can see how some of this still applies to me today. Thankfully, I seem to have calmed down as I got older, though. I do occasionally think about doing some of those things, but I don't actually do them.

What was I thinking…?

What would Noah think if he knew? Would he judge me? Would he think that maybe he got involved with the wrong kind of person?

I ask that last question because he has to know that at any time that behavior could come back. I'm not cured, I'm just managing it with medication and a surprisingly good ability to mask my symptoms. Maybe I shouldn't tell him these things. But then… that would be hiding stuff from him, and I said we shouldn't do that.

I make a mental note to talk to my therapist about all this. I'll at least start with her.

"What are you thinking?"

Jessica has walked into the room and sat down on her bed.

"Oh, just about my past. Some of the shit that I've done. Some of my regrets."

"I get that," she says. "I once tried to run away with my ex's band across the country. I got into gambling a few years ago. I've slept around. So yeah, I have plenty of those."

"Wow."

"Yeah. I know. There are many reasons my family and I aren't super close anymore. Those are just some of them."

"I'm sorry," I say.

She shrugs.

"Is what it is."

She doesn't say anything more and neither do I. She just sits there in silence and I continue to lie in silence. And that's just what we do.

-

That night I have a dream that must have come from Jessica telling me she had a psychotic break, because in this dream I'm experiencing my own sort of mental break down. I'm screaming and crying and throwing things at people and accusing them of ridiculous shit. I'm arguing with my family, telling them that I know they all hate me and that they only feel obligated to pretend they don't.

My family screams back. We're in a screaming match. It's all of us. Four on one.

I wake up sometime in the middle of the night, sweating. I've soaked through my pajamas. Now I can't get comfortable because I'm damp and my heart and my mind are both racing. The dream felt so real.

The scariest part of all, though, is that the feelings that were inside me in that dream have been inside me before while I was awake. I've just never acted on them. But sometimes… sometimes I just want to scream and rip my hair out and completely lose my shit. It's possible that dream could become a reality if I'm not careful.

Chapter Forty-Six

I'm tired in the morning, but I still get out of bed at my normal time and head to take a quick shower before breakfast. After breakfast I play card games with some of the other patients. I get my ass kicked every single time, no matter the game. Clearly these people have had more time to practice than me.

After that I decide I will read a book. I get twelve chapters in before I put it down and go back to bed to lie down. I'm not looking to take a nap, I just need to close my eyes and breathe for a moment. Plus, I'm kind of bored of doing the same things.

I know, I know, I'm kind of skipping over a lot of the experience here, but that's the thing. This psychiatric hospital stay is not a big focus in my story. It's really a small part of the collective whole. Also, it's boring anyway. Nobody would want to listen to me talk about all the mundane things we do and talk about. The main point is, I'm doing better.

So, how about I skip to my final therapy appointment? To sum up the other ones, they're formally diagnosing me with Bipolar 2 after everything I told the therapist. Now we get to talk about my future.

-

"Hello, Charlie," Dr. Ruby says as I walk in.

"Hi."

'How are you feeling today?"

"Better. I don't feel like life is too overwhelming anymore. I think I'm starting to feel normal again."

"That's good. I'm glad to hear that. So, what would you like to talk about today? Do you think you're getting close to being ready to leave?"

"I don't know," I answer honestly. "I want to say yes."

"You want to. But?"

"Then I think about what's on the outside and it just starts to feel overwhelming again. I don't want to end up back where I was."

"But you believe your meds are helping you, yes?"

"Well… yes… but what if they stop?"

"You'll cross that bridge when you get to it."

"I don't want to get to it."

"Who knows. Maybe you won't."

"What are the odds here?"

"I can't tell you the odds," she says. "They're different for every person."

"That's not very helpful."

"I'm sorry. We can't always predict everything, though. Sometimes, we just have to go with the flow and see where that takes us. That's life. There is the option, however, for you to continue therapy once you get out of here. Is that something you would seriously consider? It could definitely help you feel more ready to leave."

I think about it for a moment. She's right. It would be beneficial to me to continue talking to someone after I get out. I won't be as scared if I know that I still have someone to go to if things get rough."

"Yes."

"Good. I think it would help you adjust outside of this hospital."

"So… what now?" I ask.

"What do you mean?"

"What do we talk about?"

"That's up to you."

I think for a moment, but I can't think of anything. We've already gotten my biggest concern out of the way, and other than that I'm feeling pretty good.

"I don't think I have anything else."

"We still have twenty minutes. How about we talk about your family. You never seem to want to talk about them. Is there a reason for that?"

"I just don't think they're relevant. I had a good childhood. My family loves me. We're not as close these days, but that's just because we're all busy with life. Isn't that how it goes?"

"Do they know about your mental health?"

"My mom sort of does. I told her about the possibility of Bipolar Disorder when I called her to see if we had anyone else with it in the family. She was supportive."

"That's good. So where do you think all the insecurities come from? You said in one of our previous appointments that you're used to people focusing on what went wrong rather than what went right. Who are those people?"

"Mostly teachers. Some friends. Maybe a little bit of my family."

"Do people still treat you this way?"

"Well… no."

"Do you think it will be possible for you to stop seeing yourself in a negative light if you focus on the people in your life now, and how they treat you?"

"I suppose… probably."

We talk about that a little longer. I guess I never really thought about it like that. I haven't had people focusing on all my mistakes in a long while. In fact, it seems like the people in my life now only like to focus on the good things, the accomplishments. Maybe it's time to let go of my past. Maybe I don't have to worry about that so much anymore.

I walk out of this meeting feeling pretty good. Everything feels lighter, like there are no longer weights on my shoulders. At least in this moment I feel a little more free. Free to be whoever I want to be, regardless of what other people think. Because other people don't always get it right.

-

I head to the phone once it's open. I need to talk to Noah.

"Hey, Charlie."

"Hi, Noah. I just wanted to call you to let you know that things are going well right now. I had a therapy appointment earlier today and I've decided that this is something I want to stick with once I get out of here."

"That's great!"

"Yeah. I think I'm gonna be okay."

"I know you are. You got this."

I smile. Noah never stops knowing how to make me smile.

"So yeah… I'm gonna have to set that up at some point. But anyway… I kinda just wanted to hear your voice," I admit. "It's a little lonely in here. I'm not very close with anyone other than my roommate, which is good apparently. My therapist has let me know that this isn't the place to make friends, it's a place to help me heal. I shouldn't focus on meeting other people. I just… I wish I could anyway. I need people to talk to."

"I can understand that. But hey, from the sounds of things you shouldn't be there much longer right? It sounds like you're doing much better."

"Does anyone else at work know?" I ask.

"No. They just think you're really sick with some virus. At least, that's what I told them. I didn't think you'd want me to tell them the truth."

"Thank you. You would be correct."

"Sarah's really concerned."

I can imagine. That was the first time she'd ever seen me in such a low spot.

"Well… maybe I'll explain it all to her after I'm out."

"Up to you. Technically you don't have to at all if you don't want to. It's no one else's business."

"Yeah… I know."

We talk for a little while longer about how things are going in our lives before I finally have to hang up. There are three people behind me this time, all waiting for the phone. I hadn't realized I was hogging it so much. I got lost in the world of Noah.

"Sorry," I say as I pass them by.

-

Later on in the day I eat lunch with Jessica and Armani. There are a few other people at the table, but those two are the only ones I talk to. Well… I talk *at* Armani, because she doesn't respond. But still, I don't want her to feel left out.

After dinner we have a little free time before bed. Jessica and I play cards. She kicks my ass the whole time, as per usual. Armani joins us, even if she doesn't speak. We make sure to play games that don't require us saying anything to anyone else. She seems to be happy about this. There's a smile on her face for once.

That night in bed I fall asleep easily, something that hasn't happened in a while. It's great. And even better? I have a really good dream.

It's summertime, I'm with my family and I'm introducing them to Noah. They love him. I'm happy. He's happy. They're happy. Everyone is just... happy. Dusty and Nova are there too, and they get along. We're all at the beach. It's warm and sunny with a light breeze, my favorite kind of weather.

Sarah shows up too, along with a few other people that I work with. I introduce them to my family too, and introduce my family to them. Back up in the grass we have a picnic table set up with food and drinks and desserts. My dad grilled like he always does in the summer. I grab a soda from the cooler and sit down in the sand next to Noah.

I hope that *this* dream comes true. I would like to experience this moment in real life. At least, I would like to experience Noah and my family and summer and a picnic and our pets getting along. I wouldn't necessarily like to invite people that I work with into this situation, not in real life. I like them and we get along, but we're not *that* close.

I end up sleeping through the whole night, though. I don't wake up again until one of the other patients comes around and tells us all that we need to get up and get ready. It’s the best sleep I’ve had in a long time.

Chapter Forty-Seven

The next day I feel really good. A few more days and another meeting with my therapist and I'm out. I have a plan to start with a therapist and to check in with my doctor, though my meds seem to be doing their job, so I'm not worried about needing to change them. I have a support network through friends and family. I have my job that I actually really like to go back to, and I know now that I'll have support there as well.

My mother is there waiting for me when I get out, as I've finally managed to get a hold of her, thanks to the help of Noah. I haven't seen her in person since last Easter, so it's nice to finally have her here with me. We take a day to ourselves and go shopping. I update her on my life and she does the same for me.

The day after that I hang out with Noah. I want to get one more day in before I go back to work. He comes over to my apartment with Nova and we take a walk outside.

Everything Is Alright

I go back to work the next day and schedule an intake appointment with a therapist after finally managing to find one who is accepting new patients.

A few more small ups and downs and I finally feel truly stable for the first time in 16 years. When I go on one of my walks at work, the whole world looks different, but in a good way. For once I'm not only not depressed, but I'm not "too happy" either, or hypomanic, as my doctor calls it. I can tell I'm going to be okay from here on out, even if there are bumps in the road here and there.

I finally explain everything to Sarah and she's actually super cool about it. Between her and Noah I have a pretty solid team here at work. I haven't told any of the others, but not everyone needs to know.

-

Once I finally start going to therapy I learn a lot. I end up learning that it is very common for Bipolar Disorder 2 to be mistaken for Major Depression, and that a lot of people go through several medication and dosing changes and combinations before they finally find what works for them. That last part I remember from before, though, when I talked about it with Noah.

I am glad I listened to him and faced my fears. That's really what got me to try bettering myself in the first place. I probably could have done that on my own, yes. I'm not saying I needed a man to get me to this point, but having support in general was a big help. I think I would have let things get a lot worse.

And I know what you might be thinking after I say that. How could it possibly get worse than sitting in my bathroom with two bottles of pills in my hand? My answer to that is simply, I could have actually lost my life, for one.

Living with this illness isn't easy and there are a lot of people out in the world who have it worse than I do. There are people who have lost jobs, friends, family, and money to this illness. It can be debilitating. There are people who have actually taken their lives. That's why I wish more people knew about it. The stereotypes in the media just don't cut it. Everyone's experience is a little different. I'm just glad mine has had a relatively low impact on my life.

Honestly, I wish this country was better with mental health in general. Sure, we have come a long way in some respects, but there's still a long way to go. Knowledge is a big part of that. Resources need to exist. Maybe someday, if more people put their stories out there, things can get even better. That's partly why I wanted to tell mine.

Don't get me wrong, though. I know that for some people putting their story out into the world wouldn't be helpful. I know that not everyone wants to or can tell their friends or family, and telling your place of employment can actually backfire. I wish that wasn't the case. I wish everyone had the freedom to be who they are and get whatever support they need in order to make it in this crazy world, not just in respect to mental illness either.

But I could ramble on about that forever….

-

“So, what now?” Noah asks.

I’ve already gone to work again and had a successful first week back. It’s after work hours, so now I’m at Noah’s house for the first time, and Nova is lying on the floor by his feet. It’s a cute little house, enough for a single person. It’s immaculately clean and organized, which doesn’t surprise me at all. I’m just amazed he can even afford a house in this city. Honestly, I think I’m going to end up renting forever.

“Well… right now I would like to tell you that I love you without being in the middle of an episode, so you know I really mean it.”

Noah smiles.

“I still love you too.”

“Even after everything?”

He nods.

“I could say the same thing,” he reminds me. “It’s been a few months now and you’ve still been putting up with my OCD.”

“I wouldn’t say ‘putting up with it’ like it’s something bad. It’s just different, and different isn’t bad. I understand that it can affect your day to day life sometimes and be frustrating, and I’m not trying to minimize it at all, but I can tell you that I haven't been annoyed with you. It's bad for you. And it's bad for me in the sense that I don't want to see you suffering when things get tough, but it's not bad for me in the sense that it's a turn-off or a deal-breaker. It's just a part of you."

"Seriously?"

I nod.

"Seriously."

He smiles that smile of his that I love so much.

"We'll see if you're still saying that years down the line," he says as he lightly nudges me.

"Years, huh?"

He laughs.

"That's my plan," he says. "I'm hoping that it's yours too."

"Yeah," I say with a smile. "That's my plan too."

Everything Is Alright

Kelli Rajala

Made in United States
Orlando, FL
02 December 2024

54865205R00166